STILL LIFE WITH CORPSE

The elevator rattled down and John said, "We'll have a look. Why don't you wait in the car, Cassie?"

It was a temptation, but if my future was with John, I thought I might as well start to learn the ropes. I overrode John's strenuous objections and went with them. It was just like Menard had said. The door was ajar, the apartment dark.

"Don't touch anything," John cautioned.

Then he quietly closed the door and turned on the lights, carefully, just touching the end of the switch. The artist Latour was sprawled on the floor, with a little brass knife sticking out of his back.

Jove Books by Joan Smith

THE POLKA DOT NUDE

CAPRICCIO

A BRUSH WITH DEATH

A BRUSH WITH DEATH

JOAN SMITH

JOVE BOOKS, NEW YORK

A BRUSH WITH DEATH

A Jove Book / published by arrangement with
the author

PRINTING HISTORY
Jove edition / May 1990

ISBN: 0-515-10304-7

Jove Books are published by The Berkley Publishing Group,
200 Madison Avenue, New York, New York 10016.
The name ''JOVE'' and the ''J'' logo
are trademarks belonging to Jove Publications, Inc.

PRINTED IN THE UNITED STATES OF AMERICA

10 9 8 7 6 5 4 3 2 1

A BRUSH
WITH DEATH

CHAPTER 1

You'd think when a man said he couldn't live without you, he meant in close proximity—if not in the same house, at least the same city or country. But no, it seems my fiancé's vital organs continue functioning just knowing I am on the same planet. While he capers around Europe, I am stuck in what Voltaire so vividly described as *"quelques arpents de neige,"* otherwise known as Canada. Voltaire got the environment right. He erred in the size. There must be zillions of arpents of snow. Whole mountains of it loom like elongated pyramids along the sides of the roadways, adding a further hazard to the little game drivers play here in Montreal. It's called kill the pedestrian. If you think the Indy 500 is dangerous, you should try crossing St. Catherine's some busy afternoon. I saw a motorist knock over a traffic cop at the corner of St. Kitt's and Crescent yesterday.

But I digress. John Weiss, my fiancé, is not totally responsible for my being here. I want to finish my education, at least get a B.A. Because French is my major, I'm taking it at McGill University, in Montreal. I was tempted to join John in London, where he's a very peripatetic investigator for a major insurance company. The last I heard he was in Holland. I'd only known him a short while when we got engaged, and at the time it seemed a sensible idea to wait till I graduated before we got married. I didn't know then that John doesn't write letters. Oh, he phones—long distance from London and Paris and Am-

1

sterdam, throwing me into conniptions of jealousy that I'm not with him.

The thing is, I haven't heard from him for *three weeks*, and with Christmas fast approaching I want to firm up holiday plans. In two days my Christmas exams will be over, and I haven't a clue whether we'll be going to my home in Bangor, Maine, for the holidays, or to Plains, Nebraska, to meet John's folks, or what. I could have gone to Mount Tremblant with the university ski club. I would have loved that, but I didn't sign up because I hadn't heard from John. I don't know what to get him for Christmas either, but if he doesn't get me an engagement ring, fur will fly, possibly also teeth and limbs.

All this makes studying for my exams very difficult. Before me sits a stack of notes six inches high that I should be reading. I am really not all that steady on the development of the novel in France. I keep forgetting whether it was Flaubert or Balzac who struggled over "*le mot juste.*" It must have been Flaubert. Nobody who poured out such mountains of prose as Balzac could have spent a day struggling over one word. I hope *Madame Bovary* is on the exam. I loved Emma—as a character I mean. I think she would have been a pain in the ass to know personally. But when it comes time to discuss the character, the main thing I remember is that Flaubert, despite his struggling over the words, gave her three different eye colors— brown, deep black, and blue. And when pressed to identify her, he said *he* was Emma Bovary. I wonder what color his eyes were.

I went to bed that night with a headache and a vague feeling of unease. I was alone in the apartment that I share with a classmate. Sherry Cobden had finished her exams that afternoon and gone home. With my usual stunning luck, I had an exam on the last possible day, afternoon at that. I set the alarm for seven, to be sure I made it to the university in time for my second last exam, which I did. It went fine. *Madame Bovary* was on, for thirty marks. I recognized all of the excerpts in the sight passages and bs'd my way through the comments. I was in a good mood as I ploughed my way through campus toward the bus stop, hooded head bent into my collarbone against the gale-force winds. When the wind decides to blow in Montreal, you don't try to identify the people you meet. If you manage to tell the people from the trees and avoid both, you're doing well.

I saw a hooded, huddled form slogging through the snow and automatically nudged over to the edge of the path. The hood moved to the left to take a peek at me, and I readied a conspiratorial smile for whoever could be bothered to speak on a day like this. First I could only see an Eskimo-like ring of fur, with a red nose and a large mustache peeking out behind it. The mustache reminded me of John's. I smiled.

The face peeked out a little farther. I identified brown, liquid eyes behind the snowy eyebrows, and my hopes soared. The lips opened in a boyish grin, and there was no longer any doubt. Even without seeing his hair, which is brown and just beginning to recede a little in front, I knew it was John Weiss. His smile was unmistakable, with those white teeth overlapping just a tiny bit in front. My heart raced like a jet engine, and I felt tears scald my eyes, just before they froze.

"Cassie, is that you?" he asked. Puffs of breath hung on the zero degree air. Zero Fahrenheit, I mean. I can't get used to the centigrade scale they use here.

I dropped books, notes, clipboard and threw myself into his arms, half-laughing and half-crying. He must have been doing bench lifts. He managed to get me, wearing about twenty pounds of sheep-lined suede coat and boots and a shoulder bag holding four books, into the air and swung me around.

"Where did you come from? What are you doing here? Why didn't you write?" I peppered him with questions while my face hovered three inches above his, and the white world spun around me.

John isn't one for wasting time. Instead of talking, he kissed me very thoroughly indeed. It was a—*different*—sensation, to feel a frosty mustache turn liquid against your face. I felt something inside me melt too, and I'm not talking about sensual arousal. He still loves me! is what I thought, and I have to admit that what was dissipating inside me was fear that I'd lost him. Our romance had been brief, and interrupted by a somewhat engrossing mystery involving my kidnapped, violin-playing uncle, the Great Mazzini, and a stolen Stradivarius. We didn't really know each other inside out, the way you should before agreeing to marry someone. With John's globe-trotting life, the possibility was always there that he'd go falling in love with some mane of blond hair and lithe, tanned torso on the Riviera, and forget all about me.

After a long, reassuring kiss, he put me down and we scrabbled around in the snow, trying to pick up all my junk with our bulky gloves. "I hardly recognized you," John laughed. "Talk about all women looking alike in the dark. They all look like Eskimos here. In fact, I had trouble telling the women from the men."

"Wait till you see the demoiselles with their coats off. I don't think you'll have any trouble."

We had everything picked up, and I said, "Do you want to go to the coffee shop, or back to my place?"

"I rented wheels. I thought we might go out somewhere for lunch."

"You're planning to drive in Montreal? Brave man."

"Yeah, I noticed they drive like Cariocas, and the snow adds a new challenge."

It was a great relief not to have to line up on the street corner and wait for a bus. In winter, the cold, raw wind whips up from the St. Lawrence and can freeze you solid in two minutes. People are so anxious to get in out of the cold there's a stampede at the bus doors. John had rented a blue Crown Victoria. He likes big cars. It was still warm, and I had the luxury of taking off my gloves and pulling down my hood. John did the same.

He turned and studied me from his melting brown eyes. "Yup, you're a woman all right," he smiled, and kissed me again, in a much more leisurely way than the first time. Then he said, "Where do you want to eat? Let's make it someplace special."

I noticed that beneath his Eskimo coat, John was wearing a very elegant dark suit, white shirt, and striped tie. I had thrown on a big sloppy sweater and wool slacks, with long johns beneath, which added an inch to my nether dimensions. During exams, I hadn't bothered much about such details as hair and makeup.

"Oh lord, I can't go to a decent restaurant looking like this. Let's go to McDonald's."

"You look fine to me, Cass," he said, and turned on the engine. To avoid parking problems, we went to his hotel, the

Bonaventure, which is a very nice hotel. John's specialty is recovering stolen property that his company has insured, and he makes a very good living indeed.

I felt like a poor relation in that fancy dining room, but John had enough class to cover me. When I first met him, he was masquerading as a cowboy, and I tended to think of him in that guise. He really did have a little touch of the West in his speech, but as he ordered from the French menu with no trouble, I realized he was cosmopolitan. Of course he would be, with his globe-trotting job.

I have an unnatural passion for luxury. Meretricious glamour always attracted me. Vuitton luggage, truffles, Dom Perignon champagne, anything in a Tiffany box. Thus far, these goodies are familiar to me only from the pages of *Connoisseur* magazine. You don't see many Vuitton bags in Bangor. John says I have one foot firmly anchored in a castle in the air, the other on a cloud.

We started with a Bloody Marie, which John explained is a Bloody Mary with garlic, and very tasty. "I discovered this in Marseilles," he said nonchalantly.

"What were you doing in Marseilles?"

"Recovering a three-million-dollar yacht that was supposed to have sunk off the Riviera. The guy had it painted and rerigged and took it to Marseilles to sell. He blew up a little tugboat and had some friends testify that it was his yacht, the *Stella Maris*."

I hung on every rich syllable. "How did you find out?"

"I knew from the debris it was a scam, and just took it from there."

"That must have been a good addition to your wallet. Why are you looking a little glum? Oh darn, they don't have nouvelle cuisine." I was not entirely distressed to have to submit to regular French cooking. In fact, I was smiling from ear to ear. John's life is the stuff my dreams are made of—not just the European travel, but also with an exciting job thrown in to keep it from being totally decadent and eventually, I imagine, even boring.

His lips clenched a moment, in a way that makes his mustache jiggle adorably. "I'm a bit ticked off with the company, Cassie," he said, and took a long drink of his Bloody Marie.

John drinks, but in moderation. The glass was emptying rather quickly. "The thing is, I tipped the company off to a possible crisis, and they went and gave the assignment to Jeff Penderson. Jeff's a good man, I'm not knocking him, but I thought the Van Gogh assignment would be mine."

"Van Gogh? What do you mean?"

"You must have been reading about the ridiculous prices Van Gogh's been getting lately. His *Irises* went for nearly fifty-four million, and the *Sunflowers* before that for not much less. A fairly insignificant little portrait was valued at four mil after Sotheby's auctioned *Irises*. It cost sixty thousand to insure. Do you realize the Rijksmuseum in Amsterdam has two hundred and five Van Gogh's? And there are weirdos out there who just love damaging these priceless artworks. Van Gogh's *Berceuse* was slashed a while back by some discontented artist. Insurance has become a nightmare for museums."

"I begin to see the problem. I didn't realize Van Gogh was that prolific, two hundred and five in one place."

"There are over a thousand, all told. We're only used to seeing the ones that have been reproduced, or are in our own American Galleries, and maybe the Tate. The *Sunflowers* are the most famous, of course. He did a whole series of them. You often see a copy of *The Starry Night* from the Museum of Modern Art, *l'Arlesienne* from the Met, and of course the self-portrait with the bandaged ear. He did eight hundred oils and seven hundred drawings in the most prolific decade of his life, before he committed suicide in 1890. Hundreds of them are in galleries all over Europe, the Netherlands, and Belgium and France. The security threat is staggering, and some of those museums are not rich, I mean in money terms. For the ones we have insured, I wanted to be the expert. I suggested they beef up security, and we cut a deal on insurance."

"Who'd steal them? He could hardly sell them. . . ."

"The woods are full of closet connoisseurs. Selling them wouldn't be any problem. It's recovering them that'd be hard. They'd go into very private collections around the world. It wouldn't be easy to get into the kinds of places they'd end up, with electronic security systems and guards and dogs and a lot of clout with the authorities too."

My blood tingled in delight. "Are you on a case?" I asked.

He smiled and squeezed my hand. "A very important one. Yours."

"That's wonderful, John," I said dutifully. Well, I was happy, of course. "How long will we have? We have to make plans for Christmas."

"We must do that," he said, but already his mind had reverted to Van Gogh. "I was so sure I'd get that assignment. I'd been studying all about Vincent van Gogh—I read his letters and everything. All three volumes. Poor bastard, what a rotten life he had. Only sold one painting in his whole life. Can you imagine, painting about a thousand, and only selling one? It went for peanuts. And now, when it's too late to do him any good, he gets over fifty mil for one canvas. Not one of his best either, in my opinion."

"It's a kind of lunacy. No painting could be worth that much."

"It's like anything else. It's worth what somebody's willing to pay for it."

"They must be people with more money than brains."

John had lifted his empty glass, and the waiter came trotting with another Bloody Marie. I was more hungry than thirsty, and grabbed the celery that he set aside, the easier to gulp down the vodka.

"Are you interested in hitting the slopes over Christmas?" he asked. "Some good skiing in Quebec."

"I want to go home for Christmas!" I exclaimed.

"Oh, yeah. Well, it's only the nineteenth. You could cut a few classes, and we'll head up to the Laurentians for a couple of days."

"I'm writing exams, John. If you'd let me know you were coming—and why didn't you write, or phone, since you apparently have a phobia of pens?"

"Exams! Oh shit. Do you *have* to . . . ?"

"This just happens to be my career we're talking about. Of course I have to. You were the one who thought I should finish at the university," I reminded him.

He took another swig of the drink. "I probably never would have heard the end of it if I hadn't."

I am not slow to wrath, and John is not usually bitchy. My joy at seeing him was quickly congealing to annoyance at his attitude. "Why don't they bring our food? I have to study this afternoon," I said impatiently.

John didn't say anything, but the brown eye he flashed at me had lost its puppy warmth. He sensed my mood and asked, "How is the studying going anyway?"

"Fine."

"I'm sorry I'm such lousy company. It's just that I was really hot on the Van Gogh thing. It would have meant we could more or less settle down, somewhere in the Netherlands probably. I wouldn't have to be jauntering all over the world. I'm getting a bit tired of it. The glamour wears thin after you've circled Orly or Dorval or Leonardo da Vinci airport for the umpteenth time. You begin to wonder just what the hell you're doing, living half your life in the clouds, and the other half chasing after crooks."

"The Netherlands!" I said weakly. When I dream of our future life, I assure you it does not involve dikes or tulips. It was those disparaged trips to Paris and Rome that whetted my appetite. "Holland, huh? How nice. I'm studying the wrong language."

"The Hague's a nice, clean city."

"Clean, yes." Cleanliness I could get at home. I picked up my glass and drained it, and lifted it for a refill.

He studied me carefully. "You don't like it."

"Not much."

"What is it that's turned you off?" I watched with amazement as his face stiffened, and his eyes took on a look of some negative emotion. "Is it another guy?" he asked, in a hard, don't give a damn voice, that didn't fool me for a minute.

"No, silly. It's Holland." He gulped noiselessly, his jaw unstiffened, and a quiet little smile lifted his lips. Not anger then; it had been fear. "Couldn't Paris be your basis of operation? You said Paris had Van Gogh's too. And anyway, Jeff got the job you said."

"Yes, Jeff got the job, so we can forget about the Hague. Oh good, here's our food."

The beef, simmering in a wine and mushroom sauce, melted in the mouth. The snowpeas were just right, with a vestige of crunch, and lightly sautéed in butter and shallots. I have never had bread like they make in Quebec anywhere else. A puff of yeasty air, held in place by a crisp brown crust. The Médoc John chose to go with it wasn't bad either. I could hardly find room for the chocolate mousse. When I tell you I left two whole forkfuls on my plate, you will realize the meal was more than filling.

John scrawled his signature, hardly glancing at the bill, though my Argus eye noticed that it came to three figures. It was cheap at the price.

"It's almost worth the lethal traffic for a meal like that," John said, patting his tummy. "So, I guess I take you to your place to hit the books. Can I see you tonight?"

"You bet. What will you be doing this afternoon?"

He hesitated a telltale moment before answering. "I have a little something I have to look into."

My sixth sense received a red flash. "John, are you on a case? You said you came to visit *me!*"

"I did! Of course I did. But while I'm here, there's a guy I want to look up."

He was helping me on with my coat, lifting my hair out from the bunched-up hood with loving, clinging fingers.

"What guy?" I pinned him with a demanding stare.

"No, you're busy. You go on and study. I'll see you tonight."

"What guy?" I repeated.

"Well if you must know, he's a forger, Yves Latour by name, but . . ."

Blood sang in my veins. My ears hummed, and the portals of paradise opened a crack. "I'll study tonight. Tell me all about him while we drive to his place. Are we going to do a stakeout?"

He shook his head and laughed. "It looks like it."

CHAPTER 2

"Where does this Yves Latour live?" I asked.

"That's the first thing I have to find out. He won't be in the phonebook. Let's sit a minute while we sort this out."

We sat in the marble and plush lobby of the Bonaventure while he told me about Yves Latour.

"Since art has become such big business, there are a lot of guys doing forgeries and imitations. Of course some of them get caught by all the new analytical methods—X-ray rigs, analyzing the pigments by optical emission spectographs, infrared spectrometer. They use a laser microanalyzer and gas chromatograph–mass spectrophotometer and . . ."

"I get the idea, John."

"The company sent me on a course," he grinned. "They have lots of other complicated technical stuff. The Doerner Institute in Bavaria is one of the best, if not *the* best for that kind of work. Even with all that technology, some of the forgers still escape them."

"Can't all those spectro things tell them the age of the canvas and paints?"

"A lot of the old masters used wood, not canvas. The forgers have gone hi tech too. They pry off an old table top of the right period, and use the right pigments. Get the craquelure quality of the finish by putting it in an oven. One guy even ground up an old lead clock weight to add to his white pigment, to beat the half-life test. The guys are good. In spite of all the

10

technology, the human eye and common sense are still the best detectors.''

"Does Yves Latour do all these tricks?''

"Some of 'em. Van Gogh moved around a lot, and he was usually so poor that he used whatever came to hand. The same colors keep cropping up—vermilion, cadmium yellow, ultramarine, cobalt, viridian, but in different kinds of pigments, so he's hard to pin down. He even did some on coarse, unprimed canvas—like hessian, though he usually used ordinary primed canvas. He was a bit of an experimenter, so you can't just rule out anything of the right age.''

"His style is certainly distinctive though.''

"A distinctive style is the easiest kind to forge, believe it or not. What tipped us off is that too many 'new' Van Gogh's started turning up. Not copies, new paintings never seen before. Of course Vincent was prolific, but even *he* had his limits. Latour started with sketches. Sold half a dozen, then struck out into oils. That's where they caught him. They found impurities in his reds. He escaped Europe a step ahead of Interpol's Art and Fraud Squad and skipped to North America. The guy's a Belgian, incidentally.''

"Like Hercule Poirot.''

"Yeah, and about that cagey. But he doesn't speak English, just French and Dutch, so we figured he came to the biggest French-speaking city outside of Europe, Montreal.''

"Where does your company come into it?''

"We took a hosing on Latour. Two of his forged drawings were stolen shortly after they were bought. We have reason to believe Latour 'sold' them to a friend, who arranged to have them stolen, and they split the hundred thou we paid in insurance. So I'm here to find Latour and whop a confession out of him, and make him promise not to be a bad boy again. If he pulled his sell and steal act on paintings instead of just sketches, we could be in big trouble.''

"And of course you're here to see me,'' I reminded him with a sapient eye.

"Hey, that's the main reason. But while I'm here . . .''

"Let's find a phonebook.''

"He won't be listed as Yves Latour. What we'll have to do

is hit some galleries and find out who's been trying to peddle some Van Goghs.''

"Let's try the phonebook at least. Maybe he's anglicized his name to Tower. That's what Latour means.''

"It's worth a shot."

Incredible as it seems, there was a Y. G. Tower on Côte des Neiges. John said Yves's second name was Gerard. He had the car brought around and I directed him up the mountain to Côte des Neiges. The name seemed particularly suitable that day. It looked like a snow coast. I peered out the car window for numbers while John set his jaw to the precarious task of driving in the snow, in Montreal's lawless traffic. As we drew near, we realized Latour lived in one of the apartment high-rise buildings, which made it possible for us to park in the visitors' parking lot. We pressed half a dozen buttons to get into the building. Y. G. Tower was on the seventh floor, apartment 5. We took the elevator up and began looking for his door.

It occurred to me that a forger might keep a gun, and when he found himself in imminent danger of arrest, he might use it. "Do you have a gun?" I asked John.

He patted his pocket and grinned. "I never leave home without it. But I don't think we're going to visit Yves yet. I'd like to get in and have a look around first. It might be interesting to see who he's forging these days."

"You can do that after you arrest him."

"I'm not a cop, and I'd just as lief we keep the fuzz out of this, for the time being at least. I want a nice leisurely look around, which I won't get if Yves puts up a fight. If what I find is interesting, I'll call in the A and F boys. For that matter, we don't even know Tower is Latour."

"What do we do if he's at home?"

He took a cigarette lighter and a package of cigarettes out of his pocket. John doesn't smoke, so I knew he was up to something. "A camera?"

"My Bic Pic," he grinned, and lit it. It really was a lighter too. "I'll get a shot of Yves for my own personal files. When he leaves, we'll come back and search."

We were checking out the apartment numbers as we went along the hall. "It must be around that corner," I said. "We can't just lurk around the hall for hours on the chance that he'll come out.''

John stepped up and tapped on the door. ''The French I hear on the street here isn't much like the French I know. In case Latour speaks the local lingo, you'd better talk to him.''

''What will I say?''

''Wing it.'' I stared in mute horror. There were sounds behind the door. ''You can ask him if he's interested in donating to the orphans' overcoat fund,'' John said, taking out a cigarette and readying his Bic Pic.

''You've got to be kidding!''

Before we had time for argument, the door opened and a friendly looking man said, *''Bonjour. Puis-je vous aider?''* He didn't speak the local patois. And of course he didn't speak English. My French was coming along, but I felt so foolish I didn't want to dun him for money. To stall for time, I said, *''Parlez-vous anglais, Monsieur?''*

I saw John stick a cigarette between his lips, take aim and light it. *''Un peu,''* the man said, still smiling. He really seemed very nice. He had a lot of curly hair, dark brown, streaked with gray. I thought he was about thirty-nine or forty. The hair nestled on his forehead, and clung to his neck. He wore a mustache not unlike John's, which is full and untrimmed. The outfit he wore was slightly Bohemian, which supported the artist theory. His loose purple shirt was embroidered in the front, vaguely suggestive of the sixties.

Confusion made me nervous, and I stammered out a foolish question in franglais about wanting his views on the commercialization of Christmas for my university newspaper. He asked me what university I attended, and of course I said McGill.

''Ah, c'est bon. Mes élèves ne sont pas si belles,'' he smiled, including John to avoid the idea he was hitting on me. *''Je suis professeur à l'Ecole des Beaux Arts.''*

John lit his cigarette again, for good measure. The man went on to say that he was just on his way to class, but if I was doing a survey, I could put him on the side of the angels as deriding the degradation of a holy feast to a money-spending spree. ''Adults are old enough to realize the meaning of Christmas is love, not commerce.''

I said, *''Merci beaucoup, Monsieur,''* and we left.

Once the door was closed I turned in excitment to John and whispered, "He teaches at the Beaux Arts, John! It's got to be Latour."

"Of course it is. The guy's as phony as a three dollar bill. Funny he gave himself an English name, when he doesn't speak the lingo. His accent sounded European, didn't you think?"

"It sure wasn't *joual*."

We headed to the elevator. "What's *joual*?"

"That dialect you hear in the streets. It's the French-Canadian accent, kind of like English Cockney, or American Brooklynese."

"Funny name they chose for it."

"It's the way they pronounce *cheval*."

"So you're learning to speak horse?" he asked, and laughed.

"Only incidentally. That's not what they teach at McGill. It looks as though this is your chance to get into Latour's apartment. He said he was leaving for a lecture."

John looked cagey. "That's what he *said*. It might be worth following him. If he *is* going to a class, we'll have time to come back and search. If he got the idea I was doing more than lighting a cig, he might have been lying."

"Why should he be suspicious?"

"Don't they teach Shakespeare at that college? 'Suspicion always haunts the guilty mind.' He took a pretty good look at us." John butted the cig in the ashtray by the elevator door and we went downstairs.

"I thought he was nice," I said.

"That wouldn't be because he thought you were *belle*, would it? Crooks are often nice—friendly, I mean."

"His views on Christmas too—he didn't sound like a money-mad sort of person."

"He gypped the company out of a hundred grand," John said firmly, and we went to wait in the car.

In about ten minutes, Latour drove out of the parking garage in the back. He was wearing a felt cap and driving a very nifty little new Jag. Not many of my professors could afford wheels like that. We followed him to the Ecole des Beaux Arts. When he parked and went inside, we figured he'd told the truth about that anyway and hustled back to his apartment.

"How are you going to get in?" I asked.

"If I can't jimmy the lock, I'll use this." He flashed a Royal Canadian Mounted Police badge at me. I imagine there was also an FBI and Scotland Yard and other police badges in the wallet as well.

"The janitor'll tell him he was searched," I warned.

"We'll cross that bridge if we come to it."

We didn't come to it. When we got back to Côte des Neige, we got into the building by the same ruse as before, and John jimmied the apartment door with a piece of hardware called a spider. The apartment looked innocent, with the sort of stuff you'd expect in a well-heeled bachelor's pad. There was a brown leather sofa, a wall of stereo equipment, and a lot of books. The original abstract expressionist painting on the wall wasn't bad, but it didn't give any impression it had been done by a genius. The minute we were in the door, I could smell the paints and turpentine. John followed his nose to the studio. It was a two-bedroom apartment, with one room turned into a studio.

I followed him and looked around the room. It had the usual stuff, an easel, tables with supplies and pots of brushes standing in turpentine, a linoleum over the carpet to protect it. There were paintings standing against the walls of the room. They were in the same style as the one in the living room. The backgrounds were white, with angry slashes of color laid on with a wide brush. Some of them were red and black and yellow, a few had blue and green. All were signed Tower. I cocked an eyebrow at John. "Van Gogh it ain't."

"Window dressing," he said curtly, and pointed to the easel. Beside it there was a table with a slide projector and a metal measuring tape. On the far wall, there was a screen to receive the image. Sean flicked the switch and a picture appeared on the screen. It was a Van Gogh of a seated woman in a white dress with brownish hair. At least it looked like a Van Gogh, one I had never seen before. In daylight, the colors were washed out, but it certainly had the unique tortured brushstroke of Van Gogh.

"Mademoiselle Gachet," John said. "The original's in the Van Gogh Museum in Amsterdam. She was his doctor's daughter, and the love of Vincent's life. Latour's forging all right. The goods have got to be here somewhere."

We began lifting the top row of abstracts lining the walls to peer beneath. He lifted out a portrait of a young redheaded woman, and another of a grizzled old man. "This is more like it!" John exclaimed.

We examined them, and it was true they showed more talent than the angry slashes of color. I mean you could tell the artist really could paint, but these two bore no resemblance to Van Gogh. The woman wasn't a real beauty, but Latour had made her look like a Pre-Raphaelite madonna, with a pale face and streaming hair.

"Keep looking," John said. "I'm going to scan his bedroom. People always hide valuable stuff in their bedrooms."

I discovered what I thought might be an effort at forging a Kreighoff, an old Canadian painter who was beginning to sell for interesting dollars. It was a winter scene of a horse-pulled sleigh cutting through the snow. I went to tell John, and found him on his knees.

"Say one for me while you're down there," I called from the doorway.

He looked over his shoulder, and I knew by the wicked gleam in his eyes that he had found the mother lode. I hurried forward and watched as he turned over the paintings, one by one. They were done on stretched canvas, unframed. The canvas wasn't white around the edges, but well weathered, to pose as nineteenth century. It was almost impossible to believe that what we were looking at was not the work of Vincent Van Gogh. The peculiar, twisted brushstrokes were there, the vibrant colors, even the subject matter: a sailing boat, a green room with a yellow chair, an old man with a pipe, the woman we had just seen on the screen. John kept turning. On the bottom, there were some in Van Gogh's earlier dark and austere style, like the famous *Potato Eaters*, done before he fell in with the Impressionists in Paris. There were three in that style. John pulled out his Bic Pic and started snapping pictures.

"They look brand new. They wouldn't fool anyone," I pointed out.

"They would by the time he's finished with them."

We had been there quite a while, and I was becoming nervous. "Looks like it's time to call the Arts and Fraud Squad," I reminded him.

"Maybe," John said, and continued shifting the pictures and snapping them.

"What do you mean, 'maybe'? You've got him red-handed."

His eyes glittered like diamonds. I had never seen him so excited. "It isn't forgery till he tries to sell them as originals. We're dealing with more than a minor league forger here, Cass. I think we've stumbled into something big."

"He seems to be going into retail forgery. Let's get out, John. He might be back soon."

"Right. Take a look around and make sure we didn't leave any clues. I just want to have a quick rifle through his desk."

John arranged the paintings carefully and returned them to their resting place under Latour's bed. I quickly rearranged the paintings in the studio and checked the apartment while John went through the desk in the bedroom. In about three minutes he came out, still glowing with success. He looked as if he'd just won the state lottery.

"Let's get out while the getting's good," he murmured.

We checked the peephole in the door for traffic in the hall. It was empty, and we left. I swear John was trembling with excitement. His hands were shaking when he started the car. He didn't think to ask me where I lived or anything. He just headed back to the Bonaventure. I didn't want to risk an accident, so I didn't pester him with questions, but I was nearly bursting with curiosity.

CHAPTER 3

"Want some coffee?" John asked, when we went into the hotel lobby. "It's colder than a witch's ti—ticker in here. Ticker—that's heart! Witches have cold hearts."

"To say nothing of tits. I'd love some coffee, thanks."

He looked sheepish. "We'll take it upstairs. We can't talk in public."

"How exciting! I'm being invited up to a bachelor's hotel room—to talk."

"Sex fiend!" he charged approvingly. "Cream and sugar?"

"Cream, no sugar." No point trying to diet a few days before Christmas. "Make that double cream."

But he was too impatient to go to the coffee shop. "What the hell, we'll have room service bring it up. After a break like this . . ."

The excitement was still there. We rushed up the elevator and along the hushed halls to John's room. I don't suppose the Bonaventure has a bad room, but this one was something special. The hotel rooms I've stayed in are indistinguishable in my mind. The general type consists of a room about ten feet by twelve with a very noisy air conditioner in the corner creating an unpleasant draft. It is painted off-white with pictures from Woolworth's on the walls—maybe something by the starving artists, tops. The bedspread is flowered, to hide spots I suspect, and weighs about a hundred pounds.

John's rooms—a suite, which gave delightful intimations of

18

future pampering—were much larger, quieter, and classier. The draperies and bedspread were a symphony of unspotted, dull gold fabric. If there was an air conditioner in the suite, it performed discreetly. We went to the little sitting room, which had a fridge and small table and sink as well as a sofa. I threw my books on the table and wiggled out of my coat while John ordered coffee.

"All right, tell me! I'm bursting with curiosity," I said, when he came back.

He was too restless to sit down. He paced the room, showing off his nice broad shoulders and lean torso, which looked very good in that Savile Row suit. "Like I said," he began, with his customary disregard for the fine points of grammar, "I've been swatting up on Van Gogh. I have to verify it, but if all those pictures Latour was forging aren't from the Van Gogh Museum in Amsterdam, I'm a wallaby's uncle."

I blinked, and latched on to a totally irrelevant point. "Have you been to Australia lately, John?"

He scratched his neck and gave me a rancid look. "How did you know Penderson got the Ashton case in Sydney?"

"I didn't."

It was unsettling that I had to ask my fiancé such questions as had he been to Australia. His unhappy answer bothered me not a whit. That rancor was for Penderson, not me. But we would have our argument later. I thought about the Van Goghs all being from the same museum, and soon connected it to earlier worries about insurance. "Good lord! Do you mean Latour plans to knock off a whole museum!"

"I don't know what he's up to, but it's something big." I saw that what I had taken for simple excitement contained a large part of frustration as well.

"I see what you mean. He wouldn't be forging copies if he meant to steal just the originals. What he must have in mind is substituting the fakes. That seems like a roundabout way to steal a billion or so dollars."

"A billion? Make that about five billion."

"If he could get into the museum undetected when no one's there, why be so obliging as to substitute fakes for what he steals?"

"It beats me. Unless he plans to knock off more than one

museum, and doesn't want the first one to be detected.''

I swallowed. "Wow! When you said big, you weren't kidding.''

"It's humungous. A hell of a lot bigger deal than Latour was ever involved in before. He certainly isn't in this alone. Nobody would think that big, to knock off the entire collected works of a famous painter like Van Gogh. No, it's just the Amsterdam collection he's after. And even for that, he'd need inside help. There's got to be a guy connected with the museum in on this one.''

"You said there were two hundred plus pictures there. Latour only had about ten, didn't he?''

"Exactly ten. And not actually the ten best either. I mean any old Van Gogh is worth a mint nowadays. Michelangelo's grocery list went for fifty thou a few years ago, and Vincent's laundry list would be worth something. But if Latour's forging, why not forge the most valuable paintings? He copied some of the smaller, less valuable ones, some not from Vincent's most favored period, toward the end of his career.''

"Maybe he just painted the ones that were easier to forge, and plans to sell them.''

John shook his head. "No, if he meant to pretend they were newly discovered Van Goghs, he would have done imitations, not dead ringers. You know, pictures in Van Gogh's style, with his sort of subject matter, but nothing Van Gogh had done before. He would have done a slightly different version of *Starry Night*, for instance. Van Gogh often did series, like the *Sunflowers*, the *Cypresses*, and the various *Chair* paintings. That's what Latour did before, in Europe. This time he wanted the copies to be so perfect that he had slides of the originals projected while he worked. He had a tape measure, to make sure he got the dimensions perfect, and he did them on old canvases. They were forgeries, not imitations.''

"So he plans to pass them off as originals,'' I concluded.

The coffee came, and John signed for it. "I've got to call a guy about a *joual*,'' he muttered.

"The Van Gogh Museum?''

"That too, but first I'd better put a tail on Latour. I'd feel like a jackass if he split on me. You pour yourself some java. I won't be a minute.''

I listened from the sitting room and heard John rifle through the phone book. "Is this the Discreet Detective Agency?" he asked. Apparently it was, because he asked to have a man sent to his hotel room immediately. After a minute, he lifted the receiver again and asked for long distance. He was calling the Netherlands. While he talked, I luxuriated in the splendor of the sitting room, enjoying the coffee and looking forward to the arrival of a private eye from the Discreet Detective Agency. This was how life should be—a mixture of luxury and intrigue and romance. And it was how it would be, as soon as I graduated and married John.

In that ideal world, I wouldn't have an exam the next afternoon. Fortunately I was up on my Existentialists. Existentialism had seemed a sophisticated philosophy to me in my younger days, so I had read about it. I had a nodding acquaintance with Sartre through Simone de Beauvoir before starting my formal studies. I'd already read Camus's *Le Mythe de Sisyphe* twice, and knew that he claimed in vain to disassociate himself from the Existentialists. If only my professor didn't include a compulsory question on the dialectical materialism controversy, I was home safe. I tended to get bogged down there. Who doesn't?

When John came back, he had taken off his jacket. I silently admired his expensive shirt, and enjoyed a mental picture of the chest (hirsute but not apish) beneath it. I was feeling amorous, and thought we might enjoy some romance before the detective arrived. I knew the gleam in John's eyes had a different origin and asked politely, "Did you learn anything from Amsterdam?"

Instead of answering, he put his head back and laughed like a hyena. "We've got it! The Amsterdam connection."

I felt a surge of adrenaline that had nothing to do with John's physique. "Somebody from the museum? Who?"

"An assistant curator named Jan Bergma."

"Do you know him?"

"Nope, but I soon will. He's in Montreal."

"Then he can't be helping Latour."

"He helped before he left, and he'll help again when he goes back—in January. He probably provided the old canvases.

He arranged a sabbatical working for the Montreal Museum of Fine Arts, to study American painting.''

''Wouldn't he have gone to the States to do that?''

''Sure he would, if Latour spoke English, and if Latour had been going to the States. Check that phonebook, will you, and see if Jan Bergma just happens to live on Côte des Neiges.''

My fingers were shaking with excitement now too, but I couldn't find any Jan Bergma listed at all.

''Never mind; he must have an unlisted phone. I can check Bergma out at the museum.''

''I don't understand exactly how Bergma helped Latour. I mean I assume he's going to replace the genuine Van Goghs with Latour's copies when he goes back to Amsterdam, but why did he have to come to Canada to do that?''

''Who knows? Maybe they're lovers. Or maybe Bergma followed Latour here and put the deal to him. Latour was here first.''

I considered this, and still wasn't satisfied. ''If Bergma is a curator, why didn't he have Latour copy the most expensive pictures?''

''That's the best part of it,'' John said, nearly bursting with glee. ''We were talking about the high cost of insurance and beefing up the safety at the museums a while ago, remember? Because Amsterdam has over two hundred Van Gogh's, they're going to sell five to cover the insurance costs. Naturally they won't sell the best ones. They've had some pressure from the States to share the wealth, and insuring traveling exhibits is rapidly becoming impossible, so they're going to sell five outright. It's all very hush hush. Only a handful of top execs in Amsterdam know about it.''

''But Latour copied ten.''

''Yeah, the choice of which five to ditch hadn't been finalized when Bergma left, but the field was narrowed down to ten— the ten Latour's already copied. Bergma's *got* to be in on it. That's as good as an affidavit in my books. After he returns to the museum in January, Bergma will do the switch, and the five copies will be sold with full authentication from the museum. Nobody's going to question authenticity in a blue-chip purchase like that. Then he sells the real originals to a private collector.''

"The fiend!"

"Your nice friendly Latour, who's on the side of the angels when it comes to Christmas wallowing in a spending spree."

I still foresaw difficulties. "But who'll buy the originals Bergma steals when everybody thinks they were sold legitimately to some museum?"

"You have to realize this whole thing has been simmering for a year. I bet the buyer was in on it from day one. There are lots of closet-connoisseurs out there who'd buy the Mona Lisa if they could get a hold of it. They don't want to show it off to the world. They're not in it for the prestige. They're kind of greedy psychos. They just want to own the thing, and gloat over it in private. If we hadn't figured this out, those originals would have been spirited off to some castle in Arabia, or Japan, or some stately home in Europe. Places like that are damned hard to get into."

I enjoyed a mental image of John shimmying up a crenelated castle wall in Bavaria, with wolves yapping at his heels. I poured him some coffee and between grins and praising himself, he drank.

"I knew this was too big for Latour to handle alone," he said. "Bergma's the brains behind it. All we have to discover now is who's the purchaser. They say that every successful enterprise needs three people: a dreamer to come up with it— that's Bergma."

"You mean schemer, don't you?"

"Whatever. The schemer, that's Bergma. A doer—that's Latour. He's really doing the work. And they need a son-of-a-bitch."

"That's the buyer? Why do you choose him for the son-of-a-bitch?"

"That kind of wealth is obscene. If those rich guys weren't so greedy and selfish, nobody'd steal priceless objets d'art that belong in museums. We'll get him too before this is over. We're going to play this one real cool. No cops. Let Latour and Bergma think they're getting away with it, and nab the three of them when the deal goes down."

After we had talked about all this for a little longer, there was a tap at the door. "That'll be the P.I.," John said.

I didn't plan to miss a minute of this, and followed him to

the door. Led astray by movies and TV, I had pictured some glamorous Humphrey Bogart–type private eye, drinking his booze out of a bottle and talking out of the side of his mouth. What greeted us was a completely undistinguished-looking man in a rumpled suit and hooded jacket. He was short, middle-aged, with snuff-colored hair and dark eyes. What came out of his mouth when he spoke was the local *joual*, of which I understood about two words in ten. His name was Monsieur Menard, and he was from the agency.

"Do you speak English at all?" John asked.

"*Mais oui, certainement.* I speak Engleesh good like *français.*"

"That's great," John said, and drew him into the room. He wrote down Latour's address and description, our hotel room number, and told him he wanted Latour followed, but very discreetly.

"We are deescreet—the Deescreet Detective h'Agency. This Latour, he's playing around with your woman—wife? You got the picture of her?"

"No. No wife. Just follow him. Get pictures of anybody he meets. I want time and place. *Comprenez?*"

"*Wye.*" *Joual* for *oui* is *wye*.

"Never mind why," John said. "Just tail him, real close."

"It's okay, John. He said yes," I explained, and smiled apologetically at M. Menard.

John looked embarrassed and said, "Oh, I see. Well, *merci.* Call me here. I may not be here all the time, but you can leave a message by phone."

"*Wye.* I stick with him like the glue."

M. Menard left. It was already after four o'clock, and loathe as I was to leave, I *did* have to crack the books. I reluctantly put on my coat. Then, when it was too late, John turned romantic.

"You're not leaving!" he exclaimed.

"I have an exam tomorrow afternoon, a toughie. Existentialism. But it's my last one. We really have to talk about the Christmas holidays, John."

He drew me into his arms, snuggling his hands under my

coat, and rubbing his whiskered lips against my cheek. "Existentialism, huh?" he murmured, in a tone that had nothing to do with philosophy. "Sure I can't convince you to . . ."

"Don't tempt me. Give me four hours."

He glanced at his watch. "That'll be just about dinner time. Why don't you study here, and . . ."

Quite apart from the fact that my books were at my apartment, I knew how much studying I'd get done if I stayed. "I'll take the subway home, John. Don't bother driving me. You probably have some scheming to do."

"There are a couple of guys I have to call. I better get in touch with the office. I might just give Parelli a toot as well. I don't want to get all tied up with badges, but I could use an unofficial pipeline. It's Christmas, and he might have a few days off. He works out of Toronto, but his home's in Montreal. Some backup will come in handy, since there are at least three guys to contend with. You remember Gino Parelli? He was a nice guy."

"The Mountie?"

"That's right, the guy that helped me catch Ronald. I'm sure you haven't forgotten your old friend, Ronald." He challenged me with a laughing eye.

Ronald was the SOB who kidnapped my uncle and tried to get the Stradivarius in Toronto last summer. He was a boyfriend before that. John was always a little jealous of him.

"How could I forget Ronald? So handsome," I sighed.

"And so stupid."

"I'll meet you here around eight-thirty," I said.

"Take a taxi, will you? I don't want you on the subways after dark."

"This isn't New York, you know."

Knowing my love of luxury, he said, "Are you okay for dough?" His hand was already sliding toward his wallet. "I don't want to step on any feminist toes, but we *are* engaged."

"I'm okay. Since you're feeding me, I can afford taxi fare. See you."

He came to the door with me, kissed me again, and I left reluctantly to hotfoot it to the Metro station. Actually coldfoot it would be a more appropriate word. A bitter wind had blown down from the North Pole while we were indoors. It laughed at my pitiful attempts at holding it off. Sheepskin and suede didn't begin to do it.

CHAPTER 4

As I studied, I came to the conclusion that Existentialism wasn't for the nineties, or if it was, it showed us a very sad picture of mankind. In that philosophy, there is no ideal man or human nature or God. We're each in it alone, in our discrete time and place, destined to define humanity by our actions. Human nature is the sum total of human actions, always in the making, never established. And in the last few decades, we were writing a sorry definition of mankind. It seemed ironic that the lifeworks of a die-hard idealist like Van Gogh should become the prey of robbers and criminals.

I tried to concentrate on my work, but "the case" was always there, at the periphery of my mind. So was John. I was happy he was here, even if he hadn't come specifically to see me. Would he have called if he hadn't been coming? For three weeks he hadn't bothered to pick up the phone. Even if I could afford it, which I couldn't, I couldn't call him because I never knew where he was. I was going to get this situation straightened out before he left. His work was dangerous. He could be dead, floating in a canal in Amsterdam or in the Seine, and I wouldn't even know it till his bloated body was fished out of the water. Or almost as bad, he could be with another woman.

I wanted to tie that down too. Was he seeing other women? We hadn't discussed it. I didn't sit home every night, but I made it a point never to go out with the same man more than twice. It was so easy to meet men at the university that this was no problem. With John though, he'd probably only meet one or two women in any city he happened to be in. Was he having little flings in various capitals? Was that what accounted for those occasional weeks that passed without a phone call? Tonight, for sure, I'd get an answer.

I wanted to look ravishing enough that he desired no one but me, and to this end I set aside the books early enough to put on all the bells and whistles. The Montreal ladies turn out in high style, very cosmopolitan. I guess it's the French influence. I had totally flattened my wallet on a chic little black, pencil-thin dress with long, tight sleeves. It cried out loud for diamonds, but had to make do with a chunky, modern necklace. Not even gold-plated, but in the dark, who'd know the difference? I consoled myself that I'd seen Diana Vreeland wear one of a similar design on TV.

As it was too late to visit a hairdresser, I piled my tawny mane up on the back of my head and used Sherry's hair curler to curl a few dangling strands, to soften the look. Romantic was the effect I was striving for. Maybe I should have settled for dramatic. It's hard to make an angular, square-jawed face look romantic. At least my nose was straight, and my lips full. A hint of silvery eyeshadow glitzed up my dark eyes. A smear of rouge and I was ready. My fingers encountered a little bump as I rubbed the rouge in. With seventeen square feet of skin on the human body, did that incipient pimple have to choose my face? I rubbed again, and thank heavens it melted. It was just a lump in the rouge.

Next I tiptoed to Sherry's bureau and "borrowed" a dash of her Giorgio. I didn't figure this decision was doing mankind any irreparable damage because I would have done the same if she'd been in her room. I used her beauty aids; she used my books and picked my brain. Although she attended the university, she didn't believe in wasting money on books. She was an old-fashioned girl, there for a husband.

On those rare occasions when I had a fancy date, it was understood I wore her second-best coat, a long black, fitted wool with a huge black fox collar. I feel like a Russian princess in it, and besides it's as warm as toast. Actually it looks a lot better on my long, lean frame than it does on Sherry, who has less height and more curves. I was happy to see, when I went to the closet, that she'd worn her beaver home for Christmas. I slid into the black coat and called a cab. There was an air of tingling excitement flaming through me.

A few heads turned as I strode through the hotel lobby. The heady fumes of Giorgio wafted toward my nostrils in the elevator. I felt sorry for the middle-aged, middle-class couple who shared the space with me. They had probably already had their dinner, and were going back to their room to watch TV. I think the woman took me for a call girl. She looked at me out of the side of her eyes in a condemning way and pursed her lips. I ignored her, and stifled the urge to wink at her husband.

A bright smile was in place as I tapped on John's door, knowing I looked good. He'd sweep me into his arms and kiss me. He answered at the first tap and pulled me into the room. He was still wearing the same shirt and tie he'd worn that afternoon. It was hard not to notice that his hair was sticking up, indicating that he'd been reefing his hands through it. And of course that he didn't pull me into his arms was the biggest disappointment of all.

"You're late! Where have you been?" he asked impatiently.

I knew then that the evening wasn't going to go the way I'd planned. "What's happened?" I demanded.

"Latour's been murdered."

I felt as if I'd been kicked in the stomach. I couldn't grasp it, and even when I could, I couldn't quite believe it. It was my first brush with murder. "What!"

"You heard me right. I had a call from Menard fifteen minutes ago. I should have left then. I thought you'd be here any minute." He grabbed his coat and rushed me out the door.

There were people in the elevator, so we couldn't talk. It left me time to think about poor Yves Latour. He had seemed such a nice, friendly man. A forger and a thief, of course, but personable. Even a thief shouldn't have his life snuffed out, especially just a few days before Christmas. I wondered what a man like that would do for Christmas, in a different country from his family and friends.

John must have called for his car earlier. It was waiting for us at the front door. In fact, I had a vague memory of seeing it there when I came in. We got in the car and he headed into the night traffic. St. Catherine's Street looked like a fairyland, with all the Christmas lights and decorations and shoppers. The stores were open late during this season. It brought vividly to mind Latour's condemnation of the money-spending spree. But he wanted his piece of the money too, enough to break the law to get it. He had added his cubit to the definition of humanity. And now someone had added a blacker one; someone had murdered Yves Latour.

In store windows, mechanical elves hammered on toys, and a fat, red Santa Claus's head nodded up and down as he patted his bulging stomach.

"It must have been Jan Bergma," I said.

"That's what I figure," John agreed. "He waited till Latour had done the ten paintings; then plugged him. He doesn't need Latour for the switch in Amsterdam. Now I'll have to tell the cops. Any hope of secrecy's blown wide open."

"I suppose Menard's called them already. Where are we going, to the police station?"

"Menard called me first. I want to have a look at Latour's apartment before the cops get there. If the paintings are gone, then it was Bergma for sure. But if by any chance they're still there . . . Well, then it's a whole new ballgame. Latour might have been killed for some other reason. He could be dealing a bit of dope or something. I'll have to figure out a way to let Bergma think the pictures are safe, not discovered. I figure we could stash them some place at that Beaux Arts where Latour works—worked."

"You should call the police, John."

"I will. Waiting ten minutes isn't going to bring Latour back to life. If Menard's hanging around in front of the apartment building, it means nobody's reported the murder yet. If he's gone, then the cops are inside."

"How did Latour die? I mean you said murder, but was he shot or what?"

"Menard said a knife." I felt a little wave of nausea rise up inside me. "Poor bastard," John said. "Right before Christmas too. He was such a talented artist. If only he'd stuck to doing his own work. But no. I was talking to another forger in Amsterdam last week. He was good too, and I asked him why he copied. He said 'Inspiration without skill can create art. Cézanne was a clumsy painter. But skill without inspiration is mere craftsmanship. A cruel joke of God. I lack the fire of inspiration. I am a craftsman, a forger.' I guess Latour figured he was just a craftsman too. Of course it's the money that seduces them.''

"Yes, and what it can buy," I added softly. I was no anchorite myself. I loved luxuries. I, of all people, could not condemn them wholeheartedly. But at least I'd never hurt anyone else to get money. That was my tiny addition to the positive side of humankind. Not even an addition really. Just even. I should do something positive, to add my mite to the definition of humanity.

As we drew near to Latour's apartment building, we kept a lookout for flashing red lights and blue and white cop cars. The place looked peaceful. There were a few people entering, and we spied M. Menard loitering around the front of the parking lot. I decided that his anonymous appearance was an advantage for his work. Nobody'd ever take a second look at him. He didn't say a word, but just tossed his head for us to follow him, and we stayed a bit behind as he went into the building. We got inside on the coattails of another couple, and waited till they'd taken the elevator before we spoke.

"What's the setup?" John asked. His face was white and strained. I liked that he looked so sad. It told me that despite his rough job, he hadn't lost his concern for people, for life.

Menard pulled out a little book and glanced at it. "Latour returned to his apartment at five twenty-five." He had quite a heavy accent and was unsteady in his verb tenses, but to reproduce the accent is distracting. "I check before he arrived. His apartment is on the north corner of the seventh floor. I see the lights go on. There were a lot of traffics in and out over the next hour, people coming home from work and going out for the evening. Anybody, he could have slip in. At six-thirty, his lights go out. I waited, thinking he'll come out soon. He didn't, so I thought he was visiting someone in the building. I just waited, and waited. It was getting damned cold, so I go inside, and decided to stroll up to the seventh floor. The door, she was ajar. People don't leave their doors open, even if they're in the building. I peek in, used my flashlight, and saw him laid out on the floor, with a knife in the back. So I run to the nearest phone and call you.''

The elevator rattled down and John said, "We'll have a look. Why don't you wait in the car, Cassie?''

It was a temptation, but if my future was with John, I thought I might as well start to learn the ropes. I overrode John's strenuous objections and went with them. It was just like Menard had said. The door was ajar, the apartment dark.

"Don't touch anything,'' John cautioned.

Then he quietly closed the door and turned on the lights, carefully, just touching the end of the switch. Latour was sprawled on the floor, with a little brass knife sticking out of his back. The edge on his purple shirt around the knife was darker than the rest. The blood had dried to a rusty brown. John tried Latour's pulse and said, "He's long gone.''

"But no rigor yet,'' Menard mentioned.

John knelt down and examined the knife closely but without touching it. I did the same. The handle was worked in arabesques, and there was an ornamental oval turquoise stone imbedded in it. John went straight to the bedroom. Through the open doorway I saw him lift the bedspread and look under the bed. The pictures were gone. He looked around the bedroom. "What happened to that gray tin box that was on his desk?'' he asked me.

"I don't remember any box.''

"I tried to open it when we were here before. I guess you were in the studio then. It was locked. I didn't want to tip Latour off, so I didn't pry it open, or take it. Damn. Take a look around the studio, will you, Cass?''

I darted to the studio. The box wasn't there. The pictures weren't there either. Nothing else looked disturbed. We did a quick search of the apartment, but the box and the Van Gogh pictures were gone. We didn't find anything that would indicate who his caller had been. Of course we already knew it was Bergma. He'd got what he wanted from Latour, the forgeries, then killed him, to keep all the money for himself.

John joined me in the studio. He flicked on the projector, and the familiar picture of Mademoiselle Gachet appeared on the wall. "He forgot one thing,'' John said, and took the slide. "Let's split.''

He turned off the lights and we went downstairs. At the car, Menard said, "I've got to report this, Mr. Weiss. I can keep your name out of it, but I don't want to lose my license. I'll have to tell them I was tailing Latour."

"Sure, you do that. You'll be hearing from me real soon, Menard. I'll be wanting your services tomorrow. And before you leave—was anyone coming out of the apartment just after six-thirty carrying a big, bulky parcel?"

"Lots of people," Menard said, shaking his head. "It's near Christmas. People are delivering presents, taking stuff to parties, returning things to stores. There was hardly nobody coming out empty-handed. Sorry."

"Anybody stand out in your mind; anybody look different for any reason? Worried or stealthy, maybe running?" John persisted.

"In the cold, people huddle into their collars and walk fast. I didn't notice nothing."

"That's too bad. You might be asked to identify a guy tomorrow. Maybe when you see his face, you'll remember. Thanks, Mr. Menard."

Menard scuttled off to his car. It was a dark Toyota a couple of years old, as insignificant in appearance as himself.

"Now we go to the police?" I said.

"Menard said he'd report it."

"He doesn't know all the facts."

We drove away. John stopped at the closest corner store and darted in. When he came back, I said, "Do the police want us to go back there?"

"I called Parelli."

"You should call the Montreal police. We know it was Bergma. We can't let him get away."

He took my hand and squeezed it. "Haven't you heard, the world's a global village? Even if he leaves the country, he won't escape. I'd like to give him enough rope to hang himself, and get whoever he plans to sell those pictures to in the noose along with him."

"It doesn't seem right, withholding evidence. We'll be accessories to murder or something."

"Gino's going to meet us. The evidence is still there, in Latour's back. That was a strange-looking knife. There can't be too many like that around. I wonder why the murderer left it behind?''

We were still in the parking lot beside the convenience store. Driving in Montreal isn't conducive to conversation, of course, but it was cold and uncomfortable in the car.

''I imagine people lose their heads when murdering someone,'' I said wanly.

''The murderer remembered to take the tin box. Now what the hell could have been in it? If Latour had a slide for the Gachet portrait, he must have had slides for the other nine, but I didn't see them in the apartment. Maybe there were slides in the box. There were papers too, from the heft of it. Probably his passport, insurance papers. He was using an alias, so Bergma might not want his real identity to come out. Parelli's supposed to meet us at ten tonight. He can give us a hand with all this.''

John put the car in gear and we drove back downtown. ''We have an hour to kill before Parelli gets here,'' he said. ''Do you want to eat?''

I shivered. ''No, thanks. I seem to have lost my appetite.''

''A shot of whisky would hit the spot. Are you still trying to cultivate a taste for Scotch?''

''I want something warm.''

''An Irish coffee. We'll have it at my hotel, if that's okay with you. Parelli's meeting me at the hotel.''

''Let's have it at the bar,'' I said. ''I want to be around people. I feel so depressed.''

''I'll leave word at the desk to page me there,'' he said, and I went on ahead to the bar.

It was busy at Christmas. The buzz of conversation and eruptions of laughter were reassuring after just having seen death. The demoiselles looked as soignée and ravishing as usual, but I wasn't in the mood to admire or envy them. A steaming cup of Irish coffee, larded with whipped cream, helped fill the empty feeling inside. John took a shot of Scotch straight, and sipped the soda water while we talked.

''You know,'' he said, frowning into his glass, ''I'm coming to the conclusion that Latour wasn't actually stabbed.''

I blinked in surprise. We'd both seen the knife sticking out of his back. ''Are you giving me that old philosophical chestnut about projectiles slowing down at some rate so that they never actually reach their destination?''

"And Saint Sebastian died of fright," he nodded. "No, I'm taking common sense here. What I mean is, Bergma didn't so much stab him as throw the knife, maybe from the doorway."

"I still say he stabbed the man in the back, literally."

"What bothers me is why Bergma left the knife? I think he wanted to kill Latour, but didn't have the guts to attack him. Latour was a pretty wiry guy. I bet Bergma's a scrawny, effete cultural snob. Maybe somebody was coming, so he hightailed it out of the apartment without recovering his weapon. And he was afraid to go back. The knife was still there when we arrived."

"Let's hope it's there when the police arrive. I hope it's got Bergma's prints all over it, and they arrest him."

John glanced nervously at his watch. "I hope they don't. Parelli should be here soon. I wonder if I should . . . No, an unusual request will come better from a badge."

"Men are not badges, John. They're people, who happen to wear a badge."

He looked at me askance. "That means you don't like that I'm holding out on the people who wear badges, right? Look, Cassie, it may seem kind of cold to you, but I'm not paid to find whoever killed Latour. My job is to find out what Latour is—was up to, and stop him."

"Then I guess your job's over, huh? Latour isn't going to be painting any more forgeries."

"There are ten of them already on stream. My job just changed. Now it's to stop Bergma, and find out who his buyer is."

"There doesn't seem to be any insurance fraud involved in finding out who the buyer is."

"There'll be some insurance claim in it eventually. Bergma plans to stick the phonies in the gallery to sell as originals while the son-of-a-bitch, our third man, gets the real originals. When the museums that buy the fakes from the Rijksmuseum find out they're phonies, the pigment'll hit the fan. And some sharp-eyed expert will find out eventually. The Doerner Institute or somebody will discover it."

"I suppose what you really hope is that the company will

be so impressed they'll give you Jeff Penderson's job in the Netherlands.''

He looked a question at me. "I could see right away that idea wasn't a winner. What have you got against Holland?"

"It sounds boring."

"It isn't. Trust me. My main reservation about our settling there is that Amsterdam's probably the most sinful city in the Western world. Drugs, prostitution, crime."

"Sounds charming," I said ironically. "I like glamour, not sordid crime."

"All crime's sordid, honey. I figured we'd live in the country, but close to town. Maybe on a little farm."

I fluffed my hairdo and tried to look sophisticated. "Does this look like a farmer's wife to you? I have lavish desires, John. I want to—live."

He patted my hand and grinned patronizingly. "According to *The Way of Lao Tzu*, 'There is no greater calamity than lavish desires.' "

"What does he know? Desires aren't something you have a choice about. I was born with them."

"I felt like that too when I was hot out of Nebraska. You think you're missing something when you grow up in a small town. We'll give you a few years of London and Paris to get it out of your system. I guess I can take it." He suddenly turned sober. "Of course you realize, nights like tonight go with the territory, Cass. It isn't all swilling champagne and swanking at the Ritz."

"I know. I'm enough of a puritan that I'd feel guilty if I wallowed in luxury *all* the time. I'm willing to work for it."

"I'll do the dirty work. Your job'll be keeping the home fires burning."

It was my turn to smile. Did he really know that little about me? While he was in this uxorious mood, I said, "Why didn't you call me the last three weeks? Sometimes you don't call for ages. I know your job's dangerous. I worry about you, John."

"I should have phoned," he admitted. "There was something I—I didn't want to—discuss." He looked as guilty as a shoplifter with the goods in his pocket.

My heart clenched like a fist. "What was her name?" I asked, in a thin, cold voice.

"*Her?* What makes you think it had anything to do with a woman?"

"What else would you hesitate to tell me?"

"That I was thinking of quitting my job."

My mind went blank. "*Quitting!* Are you *crazy?* You've got a *perfect* job! You'd never get another job as good as this one! You make so much money when you recover stuff."

"I thought you might feel that way." He gave me a strange look, assessing. He looked as though it was only his money I was after. I knew his dad had a hardware store in Plains, Nebraska. Was that what he had in mind? Working behind a counter?

"Why were you thinking of quitting?" I asked fearfully.

"I'm tired of running all over the world. When I learned I didn't get the job in the Netherlands, I felt a bit pissed off. Sorry, ticked off. I probably would have quit if they hadn't let me come to Montreal. That's the only reason I'm still working for them. I wanted to see you, and talk it over with you first."

"Then it wasn't a woman?" I asked. I must really love him. My major feeling was relief, not disappointment, at his wanting to quit what I considered the ideal job.

"Is that what you thought?" he asked, and looked as pleased as punch. "I hope you don't think I've been two-timing you. I don't go out with other women. What do you take me for?"

I must have looked guilty. His smile faded, and he said, "You're not seeing other guys! Are you?"

Before I was required either to lie or admit it, a porter came into the bar paging John.

"That'll be Parelli!" he exclaimed, and beckoned for the phone. Before he answered it, he said, "We'll return to this subject very soon." His face was purple. John has a low threshold of jealousy.

It is odd that a fit of apprehension should have made me realize I was ravenously hungry. Gino Parelli would be eating with us, which did not fill me with delight, although his presence would obviate a discussion of my dates. Our romantic evening was definitely not proceeding as planned. With luck,

Parelli wouldn't stay long. That was my futile hope. I should have known better. Parelli is a human burr. He sticks. In a few minutes John put down the phone and turned to me with a fierce eye. "Now, where were we?" he asked menacingly.

CHAPTER 5

"I thought we were supposed to be engaged!" he howled, in a whisper loud enough to turn a few neighboring heads.

"I thought so too. After the third week without hearing from you, I began to wonder, of course . . ." That was my sole excuse.

"So you've been dating only the last three weeks?"

"That depends on what you call dating."

"I call going out with another guy dating."

"I just went to college functions. Concerts, lectures, out for coffee . . ." His tense face relaxed noticeably. In a small voice, I added, "Dances."

"Dances!"

"Dance—one dance."

A foursome of college classmates chose that most inauspicious of moments to spot me and stop for a chat. "Oh, your dad's spending Christmas with you!" Tillie Jeffreys exclaimed, smiling politely at John, before I got around to introducing them. It was that slightly receding hairline that fooled her. Of course she's not hard to fool. I worked a few years before going to college, and I'm older than a lot of the students, but younger than John.

Things went downhill from there. My friends reminded me of the Christmas formal, and bragged about how much they had drunk, and how late they got home. Tillie didn't get home till the next afternoon. "Are you visiting Chuck for Christmas?'' Tillie asked me. I was only out with him twice!

John refrigerated a smile at her and said, ''I'd like to be alone with my daughter, if you don't mind.''

''I thought Cassie said you weren't her father.''

''She has a faulty memory.''

They left, in confusion, whispering among themselves and looking at us askance.

''You didn't have to be so rude,'' I snipped. It was one of those occasions when offense is the best defense.

''I didn't have to be gullible and faithful either. Who's this Chuck?'' He enunciated the name with disgust, as if it were excrement.

''Just a quiet, scholarly little guy who helped me with my French.''

''How little?''

''Six foot two—but thin. Well, thinnish. The Christmas formal is the first dance I went to. If you'd phoned, I would have asked you if you minded.''

''Oh sure, it's all my fault.''

''It's not a question of fault. We're civilized adults. When we're apart for so long, we can have a few dates without compromising our relationship.''

''I'm glad to hear it. I've been damned lonesome all these months.''

What future catastrophe was I creating here? ''If you like, we'll both agree not to have dates,'' I suggested hastily.

''This is going to take some thinking.''

I never thought I'd be glad to see Gino Parelli, but I was. I believe there is some height requirement for the Royal Canadian Mounted Police. Gino Parelli obviously escaped it. He is about five feet four inches of repulsive ugliness. His crinkly reddish hair is thin on top. His white, doughish face looks as if it had been modeled with a rolling pin, the roller dragged along those slack cheeks, with the extra buildup of jowly mass around the edges. His stocky body, just verging on fat, was encased in a blue suit that might possibly have some historical value. It looked as old as time. If you banned vulgarity from his vocabulary, he'd be mute. Oh yes, and he's an M.C.P. to the nth degree. I figured he must be good at whatever he did, or John wouldn't have been so eager to see him.

He joined us in the bar, pulling off a fur-hooded coat that made him look like an Eskimo. John welcomed him and reminded him who I was. "Oh yeah, I remember you now," he said, running his eyes over me. "I thought at first you were a hooker. No offense. You're the violinist's niece or something, right? Toronto, the Carpani case. How's your uncle?"

"Fine."

"I read in the papers he's back from his European tour. Did he manage to steal any more Stradivariuses?"

I squelched the urge to say, "You can read?" I did, however, say, "My uncle did not steal the Carpani Strad. He bought one that he didn't know was stolen."

"And kept it, as I recall."

"With the owner's permission." It isn't an indictable offense to sweet-talk a gullible countess into a lengthy loan.

That was the extent of his scintillating conversation with me. "So what's up, Weiss?" he asked, turning to John.

John outlined the situation succinctly. Parelli nodded, gave an occasional grunt, and then said, "I'm starved. Let's go somewhere and chow down."

"It's getting late. The dining room here is probably closed," I pointed out, hoping he'd finish up his beer and his business and go home.

"This place?" he asked, as though I'd suggested he dine in a sewer. "You gotta be kidding. This is a clip joint. We're going to Ben's Deli. The best smoked meat in the country."

John's eyes lit up with delight. "No kidding! I love smoked meat."

My taste in food is catholic, but as it happens, I hate smoked meat, even from the famous Ben's. It looks raw, and too much like a cow. I, decked out in my fancy hairdo and wearing Sherry's borrowed coat and Giorgio, ordered fattening fries and a piece of cheese cake and listened while the men talked.

I think Parelli noticed the perfume. "What's that stink?" he asked once, sniffing in my direction. "You smell like an expensive whore."

"When did you ever come close to an expensive one?" I asked.

"Are you kidding? I arrested one today—dope dealing on the side. She smelled just like you."

"You must have a sharp nose—to smell perfume over all the garlic," I replied, looking at his garlicky dill pickle as big as a squash. He held it in his hand, like an ape eating a banana, and chomped on it.

Over coffee, they began to sort out what was to be done. "So you want me to horn in on the case and see what the fuzz found in this Latour case?" Gino asked.

"I'd really like to know."

Parelli kept chomping on the pickle. "Can do, Weiss. No sweat. If what you say is right, this isn't just a local case. The RCMP'll be involved. They'll be glad for an extra badge willing to work the holidays. I'm on holidays myself, but what the hell. Christmas is a crock, right? Squealing kids, noisy toys."

"How many children do you have, Gino?" I asked, amazed that he'd ever found a woman undemanding enough to marry him.

"Me? None that I know of. I'm not married. It's my sisters— Maria, Theresa, Angelina, Gina—a dozen and a half between them. Oh and my brother Tony. He has four or five. They all come home for Christmas. Poor Ma. She'll be baking her butt off all week. Week? Did I say week? She starts in August. What the hell, it's Christmas, right? I should buy the little buggers a present."

"That's a lot of presents," I said, feeling some sympathy for the man.

"A box of chocolates. It's more than they deserve. I hope it makes them puke. Anything else I can do for you, John?"

"There are a few things. I'd like to get Bergma's address and phone number. He's not listed. Maybe you could throw a little weight around with Ma Bell. And if I'm caught searching his place, I could use some federal help."

"No sweat. I'll let you know if the knife has any prints. You don't want Bergma to know we've got our eye on him, right? No direct police questioning."

"I'd rather not tip him off yet."

"It's going to be tricky finding out where he was tonight at six-thirty without questioning him," Parelli pointed out.

"I know where he was. He was at Latour's place."

Gino shook his head. "What you got is all circumstantial. You got diddley-squat till we find some witnesses, or the pictures in his possession. If he's as smartass as he sounds, he'll have stashed them somewhere."

"That's why I want to search his place," John replied.

"They might be at the museum where he works. Finding pictures in a museum, that's like looking for spaghetti at a pasta house."

"But we've seen the pictures," I reminded him. "We'll recognize them."

Parelli turned a sharp, weasely eye on me. "*We'll* recognize them? Since when did you include yourself in, lady?"

"Cassie's with me," John said. I couldn't quite figure out whether that was an apology or what, but Parelli accepted it with no more than a disgusted shake of his head.

Gino grunted and said, "About these pictures—Van Goghs— he's the crazy guy that sliced off his ear, if I'm not mistaken?" John nodded. "Cripse, who's nuttier, him or the guys that are forking over millions for his stuff?" That last was a rhetorical question.

Hope springs eternal. I thought Gino would go home when we left Ben's. He stuck like a burr. He came back to the hotel with us after a thoroughly disappointing supper at Ben's Deli. Disappointing for me, I mean. The men loved it. I could see John was impatient to ditch him and continue our fight, but didn't like to be rude since he needed his help. At about eleven o'clock my patience gave out and I said I was leaving.

"I'll drive you home," John offered.

"Let her take a cab," Parelli said. "We got plans to discuss."

"There's no point your having the car hauled out again," I agreed. "I'll see you tomorrow." John came with me to the desk to call the cab.

"I guess you'll be cracking the books in the morning?" he asked. I thought he'd continue the argument.

"To make up for lost time tonight. And I do mean lost."

"I'm sorry about Gino, but he'll be a big help. The man's a rough diamond. He really knows his stuff, and I'm a complete outsider in this city. He's doing it on his own time too. I can't just dump him. I'll call you tomorrow morning to wish you luck."

I accepted this peace offering. "John, I'm sorry about—you

know. Those dates didn't mean anything. I just got bored, sitting around every night.''

"I guess I was pretty unrealistic to expect it.''

He had defrosted enough to give me a quick kiss before the cab left.

John called in person at about ten-thirty, which was a pleasant interruption in my studies. He was wearing city clothes, a suit and shirt and tie, and still looked wrong in a suit.

"It's colder than a penguin's tail feathers out there,'' he said, batting his arms against his body. "How about warming me up?''

I warmed him up only to the extent of one kiss. There was too much to talk about, and too little time. We went to my little living room, more or less a shambles during this exam period, with books piled on any surface that wasn't littered with notes. Even without the mess, it was only a so-so room. Sherry and I hired it furnished—cheap brown wall-to-wall carpet, uninspired beige drapes, tweedy sofa, spindle-legged coffee table, poor lighting.

"So this is where you hang out,'' John said, looking around, storing up pictures of me for future thoughts, I figured. "No wonder you're so eager to get out of it. It isn't exactly luxurious.'' That was the only reference to the argument.

"A rat's nest, but my own. Well, half my own. Have you had any news from Gino yet?''

John was grinning, which meant success. "The guy's a wizard. He found out half the stuff I wanted to know already. There were no prints on the knife. It's a fairly valuable piece, nineteenth-century Arabian. He got me Bergma's address and phone number. No answer, but of course he'd be at work. He lives in a rented house in Westmount. Gino says it's a real class address.''

"Upper Westmount is the Nob Hill of Montreal. The lower end of it's nothing special.''

"It's upper. Museum curators don't make much dough. It's kind of a prestige job, more class than cash. He's getting extra money from somewhere. I figure tonight's the time to break in.''

"Remember, I'm with you.''

He put an arm around my shoulder and squeezed. His warm

brown eyes brimmed with love. "That's not the kind of thing a guy forgets. Parelli tells me there's some kind of a party on that Bergma will be attending tonight. One of the volunteer ladies from the museum, a Mrs. Searle, also Upper Westmount, is throwing a preopening shindig tonight to congratulate the volunteer gang on this Art Nouveau Show that's starting tomorrow at the museum."

"I'd like to see that show. I've been reading about it in the papers. They have some good Erté stuff. I love art nouveau."

"You like anything nouveau," he teased.

"You mean nouveau riche?"

"I was thinking of cuisine."

"That's nouvelle, feminine ending."

"My favorite kind," he said, sliding a hand along my hip.

Because I had a mug of coffee in front of me, I asked John if he'd like one. He looked at the contents, not enriched by cream, but having the washed-out color given by milk, and declined.

"I'm meeting Gino for lunch—since you'll be busy," he added hastily. "With luck, he'll know Bergma has no alibi for last night at six-thirty. He's put a tail on him."

"Doing Menard out of a job," I said.

"I've got a job for Menard. He's supposed to be at the museum, seeing if he recognizes Bergma. If we can get a positive I.D., we're away."

I rubbed my hands in impatience. "I wish I didn't have this darned exam."

"What time's it over? I'll pick you up at McGill and we'll take a tour of the museum."

"It starts at one. I'll be out by three." I told him where to meet me and he left.

I wasted ten minutes wondering if John was really over his snit, or just didn't want to upset me before my exam. He was thoughtful like that. The rest of the time was spent trying to straighten out the strands of the Existentialist dialectical materialism controversy. Understanding this arcane matter hardly seemed relevant to real life, and I resented every moment of it. I wanted to be with John, solving the case. I made a quick grilled cheese at eleven-thirty and headed out into the cold and snow to fight my way onto a bus. It was a beautiful winter day. The sky was azure blue, gleaming in the sun. The snow crunched underfoot. There hadn't been any thaw, and it was still white. The sun reflecting off it was blinding, and I put on my sunglasses. It would be a gorgeous day for skiing.

The exam was not an unqualified success. The d.m. controversy was worth twenty-five marks, and it was a compulsory question. I figure I got twelve, tops, and hoped the rest of the exam would pull my mark up. There was a flurry of exam talk and goodbye's outside the hall as students parted for the holidays. "Merry Christmas!" "Wasn't that exam a bitch! I knew Ritchie would put on the d.m. thing. I can hardly pronounce it." "Gotta dash. My flight leaves in an hour." "See you next year!" "Are you hitting the slopes?" "Did you do Maritain or Mauriac?" "Who the hell is Marcel? I never heard of him." *"Joyeux Noël!"*

"Merry Christmas, I hollered, and flew out the door, unencumbered by books this time.

John was waiting patiently in the snow, wearing dark glasses, a red nose, and a white mustache. It had become frosted. He looked like a cross between Rudolf and Frosty the Snowman. He was beating his arms over his chest to keep from freezing solid. "How'd it go?" he asked.

"So-so. Why didn't you come inside and wait?" I asked.

"The crowd was just starting to come out. I couldn't stand the crackling. Aren't there any guys taking that course?"

"It's too tough for them," I joked. We started walking through the crunchy snow toward the car.

"Sounds like a sexist slur to me. I should complain you're not surrounded by jocks! Want a coffee?"

"I'm torn between the desire for a hot drink and getting straight to the museum. Actually there's a coffee shop at the museum. We could have coffee there."

"We're not in that big a hurry. Gino suggested . . ." I looked around warily. "He's not with me. He's doing his Christmas shopping."

"That won't take long. A box of chocolates."

"That's just for the eighteen kids. He's getting his mom a dishwasher."

"Oh, that's nice. I didn't think he'd be so considerate."

"I told you he's okay," John said earnestly.

"Sure, he didn't call you a hooker."

"Gino has the highest regard for hookers—as far as looks go, I mean. He recognized you right away, last night. That was just his idea of a compliment. He says women are usually flattered to be mistaken for hookers. The high-class ones aren't exactly dogs, you know."

"It's okay to think it. He shouldn't have blurted it out." We reached the car. "What did Gino suggest?"

"Meeting at the museum coffee shop. We'll grab a few minutes in private first, since we won't have any time alone once Gino meets us. What's nearby?"

"I don't know offhand, but if you cruise west on Sherbrooke, I'll keep a lookout."

Montreal is exceptionally well-treed and well-greened for a big city. Sherbrooke Street is one of the greenest areas. It's lovely in spring and summer, with the mature trees giving welcome shade. Even in winter it was pretty. Snow was piled three or four inches thick on branches, falling off in chunks to pelt unwary pedestrians. Some of the older buildings have gargoyles that looked as if they were wearing white fur hats. Driving took all John's attention. Scanning the business towers for a coffee shop occupied me, so that we didn't talk much. John parked in a public lot near the museum, and we went to a little restaurant in an office building.

"I'm glad we're not eating here," John said. "It smells like burned fish. These places have a captive audience. The coffee's bitter as hell too."

"At least it's hot. Did you find out anything else about Bergma?" I asked, after we were settled in.

He gave a weary sigh. "I've been waiting till we settled down to give you the bad news."

"You don't have to leave!"

His mustache lifted in pleasure, and his eyes glowed. "I said bad, not terrible. It's about the case. Bergma has an alibi."

"It's probably phony. He has to be the one who killed La-tour. Who else had such a sterling motive? He got Latour to do the forgeries, and as soon as they were finished, he murdered him, so he could keep all the money himself."

"That's the way I read it too, but his alibi is genuine. The museum had its office party last night, in a hotel dining room. He was there, in full view of everyone.''

"The party wouldn't start as early as six-thirty," I pointed out. "He could have killed Latour first."

"Nope, he was one of the two organizers. He was at the Sheraton Hotel at six o'clock, apparently making his presence felt with various clerks and waiters and sommeliers. Besides, Menard went to the museum this morning and checked him out. He didn't recognize him.''

"He wouldn't. He said all the people leaving the apartment were bundled up. He could have hidden his face with the pictures. Everybody was carrying presents and shopping.''

"It's true Menard can't prove he *wasn't* there, but I was hoping he could prove he *was*. He can't. Gino says the alibi checks out. Menard got a Polaroid shot of Bergma for Gino to flash at the hotel. They all swore he was there. It'd take time to get his car out of the hotel garage, get up to Côte des Neiges, kill Latour, and get back. His absence for that long would have been noticed. We're on the wrong track. Have to go back to square one.''

It was hard to give up this excellent suspect. He had the perfect motive. "Aristotle tells us a likely impossibility is preferable to an unconvincing possibility," I said.

"I guess that must have been before they invented logic."

"Who else could it have been? Bergma must have a cohort."

"That's one possibility. 'Evils draw men together.' Aristotle said that too. A big help to mystery writers, Aristotle. If we find the forgeries in Bergma's house tonight, we can still pin him down. But if we don't . . .'' He shrugged.

"If we don't, we start searching the museum."

"We find out who his helper is first. And if that turns up a blank, then we have to find the third man. The son-of-a-bitch, the buyer.''

"The buyer was supposed to be getting the originals. He wasn't after the phonies,'' I pointed out.

"Maybe he didn't trust Bergma—or Latour. If he got his own hands on the forgeries . . . Well, it'd give him the upper hand. Bergma's still my first choice. It just isn't going to be as easy to pin it on him as I hoped.''

"We've got to watch Bergma like a hawk. The Art Nouveau

Show opens tonight, John. Don't you think we should be there?''

"I plan to pick up the tickets when we're at the museum this afternoon. Would you like something with that coffee? I know your sweet tooth.''

"Let's save that for the museum. They have nice desserts, and we're meeting Gino there.''

We just had the coffee, and I used the quiet period to bring up Christmas again, before John could raise a less pleasant subject, like Chuck Evans. "We have to make plans for Christmas, John. Mom's dying to meet you. Would you be interested in coming home with me? We should make reservations. The airlines are really crowded at this time of the year.''

"We could always drive. It's not that far. I'd like to go with you, but I can't walk away if this case is still up in the air, Cassie.''

"I'm not going if it isn't solved!''

But I knew Mom would hit the roof if I didn't show up. Mom's a very matriarchal Italian. Our family is close. I really wanted to go anyway. I never spent Christmas any place but home. Maine would be lovely at this time of year, with glittering snow piled in mountains. Quite a bit like Montreal, really. The protective rise of Mount Royal watching over the city at the north always reminded me of Maine.

"Then I think maybe we'd better get shopping for a Christmas tree,'' he suggested.

"You really think the case will last that long?''

"It's a possibility, but if you'd rather spend the holiday with your family . . .''

"I want to spend it with you and the family, in that order. If you stay, I stay. I'll call Mom tonight and let her know I might not be home.''

"We can go for New Year's,'' he suggested as a sop.

"It's still five days away. We'll solve the case. Let's go.''

CHAPTER 6

With white-knuckled hands clenched to the wheel, John snaked through the oncoming traffic at considerable risk to life and limb, and we soon found ourselves in front of the towering gray Museum of Fine Arts. A display case in front of the building advertised the Art Nouveau Grand Opening, at twenty-five bucks a head. One of the posters would help to liven up my apartment. It was a reproduction of an Erté design of a lady in a long red gown with sleeves like wings, spread out around her.

"I doubt if it'll be sold out at these prices," John grouched.

"It's a money-raiser for the museum—for a good cause."

"I better get a ticket for Gino too."

"He'll be along, will he?" I asked, trying to control my spleen.

"If we want to get out of here by Christmas, he better be."

We went into the cavernous building, where a few antique bowls and statuettes on pedestals, backed by a tapestry, advertised the institution's wares and lured the clients onward. The east wing, where the Art Nouveau Show was to be held, was closed, but we were free to wander around the rest of the exhibits. I had been there often, and John didn't appear particularly interested in old tapestries, porcelain, and old art.

"Any idea where the administrative offices are?" he asked, while ostensibly admiring a hanging Gobelin.

"No. I'll ask at the desk."

I once again used the ploy of working for the McGill student newspaper as an excuse to request an interview with one of the curators. "Ms. James is busy," the clerk said, "but you might try Mr. Bergma."

She directed me upstair and around the corner. I tossed my head and John came trotting after me. "What, exactly, are we going to say or do?" I enquired.

"We're not going to say anything. We're going to loiter, and listen."

"You can't loiter around the administration area without an excuse, John."

He wiggled his eyebrows. "That depends on whether the secretaries are friendly."

"And pretty," I hmph'd. Chatting up pretty women is one of John's favorite ways of finding out secrets. This was to be discouraged at all costs. "I could ask Bergma for an interview for the university newspaper," I suggested.

"That'll make a good excuse to get a look at him. We won't be together. Do you want to go first?"

I certainly wanted to be on hand when he hit on the secretary, and said, "Yes."

"I'll give you five; then join you. Remember, we don't know each other."

To display my acting ability, I looked right through him and said, "Excuse me, were you speaking to me, Sir?" I went on alone to the administration offices.

One look at the secretary guarding the executive door and I nearly swallowed my tongue. I recognized her at the first glance. Her hair was not arranged in seaweed strands as it had been for Latour's Pre-Raphaelite painting, but the face was remarkably similar. The nameplate on her desk said Ms. Painchaud, which literally translates to "hot bread." How had a dainty morsel like this ended up with such a name? She looked more like a tart or, to be fair, a petit four. She was one of those dainty women, all pale skin and dark eyes, with hands about the size of a doll's. She must have been getting a preview of the Art Nouveau exhibit. Today she was done up like an Erté painting in a black dress with bat-wing sleeves, and her hair was twisted up like a jelly roll on the back of her head.

If she was Bergma's accomplice, as seemed probable, she certainly didn't look like a killer.

"May I help you?" she asked, in a dainty voice that matched her appearance. She had a delightfully seductive French accent. If a murderess had to be so attractive, she should have a voice like an unoiled hinge at least.

The phone rang. She excused herself and took the call. Mr. Bergma was busy, would the party like to call back?

When I had her attention again, I said, "I'd like to know if it's possible to have a few minutes of Mr. Bergma's time." I smiled insincerely, and gave my excuse.

She shook her head. "I'm afraid that's impossible. You've come at a bad time."

My nose quivered in excitement. "He's out, is he?"

"No, but he's very busy this morning, completely booked up, I'm afraid. He doesn't want to be disturbed. Perhaps Ms. James . . ." The phone rang again. She took the call and talked for two minutes with some dress shop about picking up a dress.

When it was settled that she would have the dress picked up by a taxi and pay for it tomorrow, she excused herself and looked at me. "Ms. James suggested I see Mr. Bergma," I lied glibly. That might make him more available.

"It's the opening tomorrow night," she explained. "There are so many last-minute details to attend to. Mr. Bergma's handling it."

The little box on her desk buzzed and an accented voice said, "Will you bring in the caterers' file, Denise?"

I duly noticed that she was on a first-name basis with her boss. Denise tripped to the filing cabinet on spiky heels and trim nyloned legs, shapely little tush wagging, and took in the file. One glance at her and I felt like an ugly, uncouth Amazon. Before she came out, John arrived. "What's up?" he asked in a low voice.

"Bergma is hors de combat, but wait till you see his secretary."

"I'll try my hand with . . ." He looked at the nameplate on the desk. "Ms. Painchaud. What does she look like?"

"Like the redhead Latour had a painting of."

His eyebrows lifted an inch in surprise. I could almost hear the gears grinding inside his head. "The plot thickens," he said. "I figured Bergma's accomplice would be a man."

"Trust me, she's a woman. We got the sex wrong. And her name's wrong too. It should be hot buns."

I hated the anticipatory grin that split his lips. "I'll wait downstairs," I said.

"Try the coffee shop. Gino should be there by now. With luck, me and Hot Buns will be along soon."

"Hot Buns and I," I said curtly, and strode away.

In the coffee shop, Gino sat with his elbows on the table, ripping into a prune Danish. "Hi Cassie," he said, with his mouth full. "Where's the boyfriend?"

"Hello, Gino. He'll be along shortly. He's hitting on Bergma's secretary at the moment."

His beady brown eyes lit with interest. "Do I smell trouble in loveland?" he asked, and laughed. "Is this serious with you and John? Are you two shacking up, or what?"

"We're engaged."

He looked at the naked third finger on my left hand. "I notice you haven't got a diamond out of him. If it doesn't pan out, give me a call." He flashed a wicked wink at me. "I'm not dumb enough to go out with a friend's fiancée. No bang for the buck there, but if you two split, and you find yourself overcome with an irresistible urge . . ."

"The only urge I feel is to wipe your nose in that prune Danish."

"Ha ha." He waggled his lecherous head. "I like a sense of humor. I once dated a chick called Pruin. Annabelle Pruin. With friends like that, I don't need enemas I used to tell her."

"You old smoothie, you."

"Ladies appreciate a sense of humor. It topped looks in the survey about what ladies look for in a man."

"What survey was that?"

"*Playboy*. I buy it for . . ."

"I know, the editorials."

"Are you nuts? I buy it for the centerfolds. Which is not to say I don't read the articles too. I read a lot."

In a thoroughly cranky mood, I said, "Really? What do you think of the dialectical materialism controversy, Gino?"

"I'm against it. There's too damned much materialism in society. Buy, buy, buy." He took another bite of his Danish and said, "So do you want one of these or not?"

"No thanks."

"I hate 'em, but they keep me regular. What's John up to with the secretary?"

"Trying to find out whatever he can."

"He won't get anywhere with that tight-assed little redhead. I already tried."

"I can't imagine why you didn't succeed."

He threw up his hairy little hands. "Women! Go figger. It's probably my size."

"She's short too," I said unthinkingly.

"Short? I'm not short! I'm small, like Napoleon. Us Parellis are all compact."

I told him that Hot Buns was the same lady Latour had a painting of in his apartment. We discussed that for about ten minutes, and then John led Hot Buns into the coffee shop. She smiled at me and Gino. John looked as though he'd never seen us in his life before, and seated her at the table across from us. I thought he'd take her to the farthest corner so I wouldn't hear him hitting on her. I felt hot acid burning me inside.

"Oh I love Paris," Hot Buns was gushing. Of course being French, she called it Paree, and batted her eyes so hard she nearly knocked off a few layers of mascara. I assumed John was boasting about his intercontinental life-style to incite her interest.

"I hope your boss—Mr. Bergma is it?—won't mind my taking you away from your desk," he said, in a good, carrying voice.

"Not when you have a Gobelin tapestry you might be interested in donating!" she smiled. "And you think it's from the fifteenth century?"

"That's what the Doerner Institute tells me."

What possible explanation could he have fabricated to have given himself a priceless tapestry that he was willing to give away? The mind boggled at his ingenuity for mendacity.

"I'd really like to discuss it with Bergma. But you said he would probably be leaving in a quarter of an hour, I think?"

Gino nudged my elbow. "That's our clue. Menard's skulking around the old dishes downstairs. We'll warn him to follow Bergma."

I rose and went out with Gino, though I was longing to remain and listen to John's performance. We made a stop at the administrative offices, as they were on the way. As Hot Buns wasn't there, we decided to let on we were waiting for her, to give us an excuse to tarry around Bergma's office for a few minutes. Gino thought whoever he was meeting might call for him. I jumped a foot when the phone on her desk rang.

"He'll have to answer it himself. I wonder how this thing works," Gino said, looking at the assortment of buttons on Ms. Painchaud's phone.

It had stopped ringing. "He'll hear you if you lift it now," I cautioned.

"He'll think his secretary came back," Gino said, and found the right button.

I heard the same voice that had asked Hot Buns for coffee, so I knew who was speaking. "No!" Bergma said in a low, urgent tone. "Don't come here. We can't be seen together. They're gone, I tell you. Whoever killed him took them. Somebody's on to us. Don't come, and don't call again. I'll be in touch with you." Then he slammed down the receiver.

"The paintings!" I whispered.

"Shit," Gino scowled. "We didn't get to hear the other voice." He hung up the phone.

There was a sound of movement in Bergma's office. Gino, that dumpy little dwarf, was extremely agile and swift as a cheetah. He had us out of there before I knew what was happening. We went downstairs to wait for John.

Of course we were both thinking the same thing. "They're gone" referred to the forged Van Goghs, and it sounded as if Bergma hadn't taken them.

"This is a new twist," I said. "Either Bergma's helper double-crossed him, or John's hypothetical third man got the paintings. Bergma sounded surprised that the paintings were gone. I don't think he was in on stealing them. And therefore he wasn't in on the murder."

"We knew Bergma wasn't in this alone, but he's in it up to his snout. He's the only one who knew what pictures were going to be sold. I'm going to find Menard and warn him not to lose Bergma. I want him closer than Velcro to that guy's coattails. He'll have to meet up with his friend eventually."

Before Gino returned, John came downstairs, smiling from ear to ear. I was almost glad to have some bad news to wipe that smirk off his face. "That was well worthwhile," he said. "Denise says Bergma is running around like a chicken with his head chopped off today. She's never seen him this nervous before a show. The guy must be sweating bullets in case the cops catch on to him."

"Funny she'd blab on her partner in crime."

"You think she's involved just because Latour did her portrait?"

I stared. "Oh no. Obviously not. The fact that she knew Latour and is on a first-name basis with her boss, Bergma—why should I let little things like that affect my judgment?"

He frowned judiciously. "Can you really see those little white hands plunging a knife into a big guy like Latour?"

"Last night you decided the knife was thrown," I reminded him, and gave the news about Bergma's phone call.

John wiped his chin with his fingers. "You didn't get a sound of the caller's voice? Not even to know if the voice was foreign?"

"Not a syllable. Bergma just laid down the law and hung up."

"It wasn't Denise. She was with me at the time."

I grudgingly granted the point. "It's somebody who knows what's going on, a helper. But the helper is supposed to have killed Latour. In that case, Bergma would hardly have to tell him he was dead, would he?"

"There could be some falling-out among thieves here. Maybe the helper double-crossed Bergma, killed Latour, and snatched the paintings. Or it could be an outsider is pulling the rug out from under both of them. Someone might have got on to them."

"Somebody like Hot Buns, who knows all the gang members," I suggested.

His grin was far from dissatisfied. "I'll have to keep a real sharp eye on Denise. Latour's murder hasn't hit the news yet, so how did Bergma know? He must have been there."

After five minutes or so, we spotted Gino scuttling forward. "Let's blow," he said. "I could use a beer right about now. Or something stronger. Got any booze in your room, Weiss?"

"I have some Johnnie Walker."

"Red or black?"

"Black. When I have to bribe a Mountie, I go whole hog."

We drove in John's car back to the Bonaventure Hotel and went to his room. "Do you want Scotch, Cass, or do you want to order something from room service?" John asked.

What I wanted was for Gino to leave, but I ordered a half-bottle of white wine to reward myself for having to put up with him, and for John's flirting with Hot Buns.

"There's not much more we can do right now," Gino said. "Menard will let us know where Bergma goes and who he talks to. I can put a listening device in his office. You might put one in his house tonight when you go, John. You'll still go, even if he says he doesn't have the paintings?"

"I'll be there. No reason to believe he was telling the truth to whoever called him. I wonder if he'll go to Searle's party, with all this hanging over his head. Maybe he'll stay home and meet his cohort there."

"Is Hot Buns going to this party?" I asked.

"She didn't say," John answered.

Gino had wandered to the counter, and poured about four inches of Scotch into his glass and added a drop of water. "By the way, I'm officially on the case now," he said. "I talked to the office. It saves me wasting my holidays by being here. Kills two birds with one stone, you know what I mean. Are you seeing Hot Buns tonight, John?"

I came to ramrod attention. John blushed. I blanched. "No," he said, "but I'm meeting her tomorrow night at the Art Nouveau do. Would you mind escorting Cassie, Gino?" He didn't dare to look at me when he said this.

Gino grinned at me like a hungry cannibal. "It would be my pleasure. You foot the bill for tickets and cabfare, Weiss."

"I have plenty of friends," I said, glaring at John. "I'll arrange my own date." Which meant fifty bucks for tickets. I couldn't *possibly* afford it. I'd have to go alone.

"Let's all go together," John said hastily. "All I'm doing is meeting Denise there. It'll look better if you have another date, Cassie. Just while we're there."

"Are you taking her home too?"

"Ahem—well, we didn't get down to details. I just said I'd

meet her there. I suppose she'll expect a drive home. She must surely know something."

"Yes, she knows how to steal my date! And furthermore, don't think she isn't capable of whipping a knife into somebody's back."

He had the gall to wink at me. "You keep a sharp eye on my back tomorrow night."

"Sure, you watch my back and I'll watch yours."

It was a thoroughly unsatisfying meeting. I didn't have Gino's staying power. I was starving by five o'clock after one measly grilled-cheese sandwich at eleven-thirty. The gourmands had had steak for lunch. John said he'd call for me around seven, and we'd eat before going to break into Bergma's house. The only bright spot in the evening was that Gino said, very apologetically, that he had to go to his sister Angelina's Christmas party that night, and couldn't be with us all evening. He'd scout out the house and see we got in all right, but he couldn't stay.

I went home and called Mom. She couldn't believe I might not be home for Christmas. "Is it that skiing party you wrote about? I hope it's not mixed sexes."

Did she think they had segregated ski hills? "No, John's here, in Montreal."

"Bring him along. I want to see him with my own eyes."

"We'll try to make it, Mom. And if not for Christmas, then New Year's for sure. Leave the tree up."

"It'll be a skeleton by then. The needles are falling faster than your dad's hair, and I paid sixty dollars for it. Highway robbery. When will you know for sure?"

"John's on a very important case. He can't leave until it's solved."

"So tell him to get busy. I want him here for Christmas. That's an order."

"We'll do our best. Bye."

"Say you love me. It's the new style. Everybody tells me they love me except my own children. The grocer loves me. My hairdresser loves me. Last week my own brother told me he loves me. Is that Victor drinking again?"

"No, I don't think so. I love you, Mom."

"Good. I love you too, and John. Goodbye, Cassie. Be good."

She would have told me to be careful too if she'd known I was helping John on this case. As far as I was concerned, Hot Buns had become the most worrying aspect of the entire affair. A man could easily find himself in over his head with a woman like that. And what did I get, a costive, runted sex maniac named Gino Parelli.

CHAPTER 7

Mrs. Searle's party would probably begin around eight. As December was drawing to a close, the sun set before five o'clock. There would have been plenty of time to get into Bergma's place under cover of darkness, search it, and still have time to change and enjoy a glamorous night on the town. Why had John said he'd call at seven, and we'd eat before going to Bergma's? If he tried to sneak away early, I'd follow him and see if he called on Hot Buns. Even if it was business, and really I believed him on that score, but even if it was business, I didn't want him lying to me about it.

You obviously can't go breaking into somebody's house in a fancy dress and especially not in a borrowed coat that might get ripped or stained. I decided to go casual but chic and wore all black—black slacks, black turtleneck. As I examined myself in the mirror, I appreciated the color's slimming quality. I looked quite quite soigné and modelish when I pulled my stomach in.

When John came at seven, he had changed out of his suit into jeans and a sweater. He did not look particularly soigné, but very sexy. John has a big chest and mannish muscles in his arms. His comment was, "Has somebody died?" but his expression was not disapproving as his eyes wandered over my anatomy.

"No, but somebody is on the verge of expiring from starvation."

"Oh." I read a question into it. "I figured we'd just grab a quick bite here. This is where Gino'll be calling to let us know when Bergma leaves."

I had grabbed about the last bite in the house for lunch, viz a grilled cheese. "I didn't buy any groceries. I thought I'd be going home right after my exams. Would you like some— uh—olives? And maybe crackers. Oh and I think there's a can of smoked oysters . . ."

His face screwed up in distaste. "Who delivers the best pizza?"

Pizza features large in my life. I had the number by heart and ordered a large, all dressed. To soothe the beast of hunger till it came, we had a beer and fought about Denise.

"Just tell me if you're seeing her later, John. I'm not a child, you know. I understand your work's important, and you have to follow any leads you have. As long as you don't lie to me about it."

"Like you didn't lie to me about dating other guys."

"I didn't lie!"

"You lied by omission. You never mentioned going out on dates. Studying—you were always studying or just going to the library when I phoned you."

"I often studied, and went to the library. That's what I was doing when you happened—occasionally—to call."

"Well to be fair," he said with a look of heavy irony, "I could hardly expect you to dart home from a dance just to answer your phone."

Before the discussion required the setting of bones and placement of stitches, I tried to calm him down. "It's nothing to freak out about. I saw a few men. You're going out with Denise."

"I'm not freaking out. I'm just a little upset."

"Charles Manson was a little upset, John. You are freaking out. And you're not only seeing Denise, you're sticking me with Gino."

"I'm not seeing her," he insisted, sincerely and often enough that I believed him. An impish grin quirked his mustache and he added, "If that's what you're worried about, I'll stay here with you all night."

I considered this but didn't commit myself to an answer.

Gino's call arrived just as I was serving the pizza. I listened in at John's elbow. "Bergma's gone," Gino said. "That Searle dame only lives a block away. He went to her place all right. His house is all dark. It should be clear for a few hours."

"Right. Thanks, Gino," John said, and hung up.

"I'll put the pizza in the fridge and heat it up later," I said. "We have time now."

I couldn't enjoy a bite, knowing what lay ahead of us. John stolidly ate his way through four slices. He was made of different stuff than I. You'd think he had nothing more exciting on his mind than going to a movie or something.

"We'll take a cab and walk the last block, so we don't have a car to contend with," he said, when we were finished.

"Good thinking." I carefully stored up all his techniques for future cases. "I'm surprised Gino didn't insist on tagging along."

"He didn't want to alert Bergma by getting a search warrant. It looks bad for cops to break in without one, so I'm doing it. I'll tell him what we find, of course."

"I'm glad to see the police have such high morals."

"We're not dealing with Sunday school teachers here, Cass."

We got out at the corner of Sherbrooke and Westmount and walked the two blocks north. A howling wind screamed down from the north, blowing us to pieces. The real estate grew fancier as we progressed up the hill. The railroad and sugar barons and financial whizzes of old Montreal had done themselves proud. Vast sprawling mansions of brick and stone were relieved from cold grandeur by Christmas lights, which illuminated without adding much of frivolity. There was an air of competition in the soaring trees, which must have had about a thousand bulbs each.

Bergma's place would have been easy to miss. It was a little bungalow, tucked in between two estates, probably originally a guest house or servants' house or something. It was set quite far back from the street with high hedges all around, and it was in darkness, which suited us fine.

I pointed out to John that we were leaving a path in the snow by tracking around to the back door, but he didn't seem to care. "He'll know we were here anyway. I don't plan to leave the pictures behind."

"He won't have them. He's not the one who killed Latour."

"He might by now. Whoever threw the knife won't want to keep the evidence. He'll have passed them on to Bergma."

John sounded so confident that I took the idea he and Gino knew something I didn't. The back door proved capable of penetration by John's magic piece of hardware. "Beats me why people put a deadbolt and a dozen chains on the front door and leave the back one practically open."

"The front door has a glass panel anyway. All a burglar would have to do is break it."

I hadn't thought to supply myself with a flashlight. Another item was added to my techniques and tool-kit list for the future. John had one, and he shone it around the kitchen. Jan Bergma had arty taste and quite a bit of money. His kitchen was red and black and white, very dramatic, very clean, and very small. There were no pictures hiding in the cupboards, which were the only possible places to hide things in that little room. The dining room was about as big as a clothes closet. It had a glass table and ornate padded iron chairs, painted white. I think maybe they were originally garden furniture. A huge poinsettia sat on the table. Again there was nothing big enough to hide the pictures.

The living room was larger, and was a suitable candidate for *Architectural Digest*. The walls were either black or something that looked black by flashlight, and everything else except the two ficuses by the windows was white. White squashy settee, glass coffee table, white drapes. Oh yes, and a red carpet with a black design. John flashed the light around, stopping at a painting over the sofa. It was one of Yves Latour's abstracts. John's smile, lit from beneath, looked diabolic. "Lookee here," is all he said, but his laugh matched his expression. We wasted a few minutes searching the built-in cupboards, looking behind and under the sofa and chairs, before going into the last room.

It was an office cum bedroom, also done in Bergma's three favorite colors. "This room's at the back of the house. We'll risk turning on the desk lamp," John said. I remembered his theory that people kept their valuables in their bedrooms. He headed straight to the clothes closet. I began searching the rest of the room—under the bed, behind and under the desk, as well as in the drawers. It was soon clear the pictures weren't here either.

John was taking a heck of a long time in the closet. When he came out and dragged the desk chair in, I was curious enough to have a look. He had found a door to a crawl space in the closet ceiling, and had hoisted it out of his way. His feet were dangling down from the hole, and I could see by the erratic motion of the light above that he was searching the crawl space. A minute later his head and shoulders appeared. He was wearing a grin and carrying a tin box.

"Look what I found amidst the bits of wood and plaster," he said. "The gray box from Latour's flat."

He pried it open. It held a box of slides and some papers. John held the slides up, one by one, to the light. They were transparencies of the pictures Yves Latour had copied, and a few drawings as well. "Nine of the ten are here," John said. "And the other one he left in the slide projector. It seems Bergma supplied these for Latour's paintings," he said grimly.

Meanwhile, I was taking a look at the papers, and found them even more interesting. "Look at this, John. It gives the exact dimensions of the ten pictures. It tells the dates when they were painted, the kind of canvases used. It says on the back of the *Farmer with Bowl of Soup* there's a sketch of a sewing basket.

"There was a painting of that!" John exclaimed.

"Painted at Auvers, April 15, while under Dr. Gachet's care. Canvas fifteen inches by twelve. It gives pigment colors."

A feverish light burned in John's eyes. "It's instructions for the forgery. Details like that sketch on the back would help authenticate that it was an original. What else does that paper say?"

I began reading. "Slide 6, Gachet's daughter watering flowers. Twenty inches by sixteen. Note bottom of skirt has green streaks. V.G.'s diaries show he ran out of yellow pigment. Mention felicitous effect of blending green."

"I didn't notice the bottom of the skirt, but Latour had the painting of Mademoselle and the flowers," John said. "These are definitely crib notes for Latour. When did Bergma recover them? Whoever killed Latour and took the paintings must have taken these too. We'll take the box, and let's have a look in the basement.''

''Maybe the murderer left the box behind. We already know Bergma was there, at Latour's apartment. He told the mysterious caller Latour was dead before it was announced.''

John frowned. ''What the hell, the pictures *might* be here, and we don't want to have to come back, so let's get looking for them.''

I took the box, turned out the light, and John beamed us to the cellar. We risked turning on the lights there too. That the basement was neat as a pin made searching it easy. Bergma had no suspicious cartons to be searched, just a set of matched luggage, containing his summer clothes. He was into white ducks and Cardin shirts. There was no coal bin. He had an enviable pair of skis and boots standing up against one wall, and a windsurf board. It seemed Jan was a bit of a jock. John scoured that place a dozen times. He even beamed his light over the ceiling and walls, looking for a secret panel. When he started searching in the washer and dryer, I called him back to sanity.

''They're not here, John. Let's move out and discuss this.''

We went back upstairs and turned out the light. We were just about to leave when the phone rang. My heart jumped into my throat, and I felt an awful urge to run. I looked at John— he was cool as a cucumber. He looked at me, hesitated a minute, and went to the phone, red, of course, hanging on the wall in the kitchen. He didn't say anything, just listened. A woman's voice said, ''Jan? Is that you? Are you there? I hoped I'd reach you before you left. Jan?'' John hung up the phone and smiled.

''It seems Jan has a lady friend,'' I said.

''She's a cute little demoiselle with red hair.''

''You mean Hot Buns?''

''Sure sounded like her to me. Of course it could have been just a business call, but she called him Mr. Bergma at work.''

''He called her Denise. She keeps popping up in all the right places to be a prime suspect.''

''Gino'll be interested to hear this. Let's go. We may have another apartment to search.'' Before he left, he unscrewed the mouthpiece of the phone and inserted the bug.

When we came out the back door, a black form that closely resembled a bear leapt out at us from behind a tree, scaring us half to death. It was Gino.

"No pictures, eh?" he said. "I have a car waiting. Let's hit the road."

Well, the car was welcome anyway. "I thought your sister was having a party," I reminded him.

"I helped her make the punch. I gotta go back later."

The car was parked illegally in the driveway of a dark house. "It's my dad's," he said apologetically when it wouldn't start. "I flew in from Toronto. Maybe if you guys could push me out to the road, I could get it going. It's straight downhill once we're out of this driveway."

"Let's let Cassie steer, and we'll push," John suggested.

"Sure. Women are equal till it comes to moving their buns," he griped, but I beat him behind the wheel. It was very hard to steer without power, but as Gino said, the motor engaged once it got moving downhill. I moved over and let Gino take the wheel, as I didn't want to have an accident in his dad's car. If it had been his own, I wouldn't have minded a bit.

"Ben's Deli?" he asked over his shoulder.

"What about Angelina's party? Won't you be eating there?" John enquired.

"Not till midnight. And her antipastos, forget it. She can't make pâté for beans. My mother now, *there* is a cook."

"I could go for another of those smoked meats," John agreed.

Where he'd put it after four slices of pizza was a mystery. We locked the box in the car and went into Ben's Deli Restaurant. The carnivores ordered their plates of meat. I settled for coffee, and felt very virtuous.

"So what did you find?" Gino asked. "I noticed Ms. Newman was carrying a box. Is it money?"

"No, it's slides," John said, and explained what we had.

"We got our collusion tied up," Gino nodded. "Latour's prints'll be on the box, along with Bergma's. And probably yours, Weiss. I hope you handled it with care. But till someone peddles the pix, it's legal. You can paint yourself up a Picasso and sign it Pablo, but until you sell it as an original, you're innocent as a lamb. Where do you figure the forgeries are, Weiss?"

"Possibly in Ms. Painchaud's apartment," John said, and told him about the phone call. "We'll have to have her followed too."

"You think men grow on trees? I'll check her alibi for the time of Latour's murder. Of course Bergma will try to cover for her. She must have been at that museum Christmas party too."

"Maybe not at six-thirty," I reminded them eagerly. "Jan Bergma was organizing it. She could have arrived later—after she'd knifed Latour and stolen the paintings."

"Women don't usually use knives," Gino said, while wolfing down his meat. "Not in North America anyway. Poison, guns nowadays, but a knife . . ." He stopped and took a loud crunch of pickle.

"She must be Bergma's girlfriend," I decided. "She works for him—it's logical. That'd explain the painting. Latour did it for Bergma."

"Why didn't he give it to him?" Gino asked.

"Maybe it was going to be a Christmas present."

"Yeah," Gino said, "but Bergma arranged to give him a Persian knife first."

"The paint was dry, and the picture was dusty," John said. "Latour did his Christmas painting early, if that's what it was all about."

Gino listened sharply, while still wolfing down his meat. "And if she's Bergma's lady, how come she has the hots for our John?" he asked, with a sly grin at me. "She must be a nympho, you lucky bastard, Weiss."

John refused to look at me. I didn't like the way this whole investigation was going. It would end up with John dating her to get a look around her apartment. I put my wits to work and said, "What we'll have to do is slip away from the Art Nouveau opening tomorrow night and search her apartment."

"She's home now," Gino grinned. "I bet you could get into her bedroom without too much trouble, Weiss. I'd be only too happy to volunteer for the job, but the lady seemed to prefer you. Don't worry, Cassie," he added with a lecherous grin. "I won't let you get lonely."

"You can call me Newman," I suggested, to cool his ardor.

"I've noticed ladies like that macho touch." He reached out and grabbed my hand, smearing it with pickle juice. "Newman it is. New man, get it? Ha ha. Just kidding, Weiss."

"We'll hit Ms. Painchaud's apartment tomorrow morning while she's at work," John said. I breathed a big sigh of relief.

"Too bad," Gino said, and winked at me. An end of meat escaped his lips and dangled over his chin. He stuck out his tongue and rescued it with a flip, like a frog picking a fly out of the air. "Ben has the best damned smoked meat in the whole world," he said, and grabbed his pickle.

I tried to ignore him. It's disconcerting to watch an animal eat. "What do you think Bergma will do when he finds his box is gone, John?" I asked.

"I don't know. Did you put the bug in his office phone, Gino?"

"Of course I did. Did you bug his house phone?" John nodded. "Then we'll soon know who he calls," Gino said, and patted his stomach. "I think I could handle another. How about you, Weiss?"

John squeezed my hand under the table. "One's enough for me." He smiled a smile that spoke of more than food.

"Maybe I better not either," Gino decided. "Angelina's serving canneloni. Her pâté stinks, but she uses Ma's recipe for her pasta sauce."

"Did you get your mother's dishwasher?" I asked.

"I did, and you wouldn't believe what they soaked me for it. There's going to be an installation charge on top of that, and the bastards won't install it Christmas eve. I wanted to see Ma's face Christmas morning." He looked like a little angel when he said that. I almost liked him, till he added, "At least my dad'll get stuck for the installation charge. Plumber *and* electrician. Ha!" He laughed raucously.

He was still laughing when he put on his parka and left. Maybe because he had stuck John with the bill.

CHAPTER 8

You're probably wondering if John stayed overnight. He didn't, and what we did before he left is not much of a part of this story. I told him I had given Mom the bad news about Christmas. We talked about the case and Christmas mostly. He absolutely forbid me to buy him a Christmas present, except a token. I didn't argue too much because money was tight with me. Of course I did the "gentlemanly" thing and insisted he not buy me more than a token either, thus banishing my hopes for an engagement ring.

I slept in the next morning and went shopping in the early afternoon for John's token. It is very hard to find a meaningful token for ten dollars, the sum agreed on. In fact, it's pretty well impossible. I had to exceed the limit to buy him a book on Van Gogh. It had plentiful reproductions and talked about the artist's life as well. I hoped John didn't already have it. One of the nice things about giving books is that you have a brief enjoyment of the gift yourself before wrapping it. And as usual, I ended up being sorry I had to part with it. Van Gogh was truly a unique artist. He invented a style and made it so much his own that even an artistically illiterate person like myself could identify his work. I could not always tell a Raphael from a Botticelli at a quick glance. Tintoretto, Titian, and Caravaggio are melded into one grandiose swirling canvas in my mind, but a Van Gogh was like a Modigliani. Nobody else could have painted it—except of course a master forger.

Knowing that Van Gogh had been in an asylum, I could easily see, or imagine, the evidence in his tortured brushstrokes. I read about his mental illness, the fits of depression that co-incided with letters from his brother Theo bearing bad news. When Theo was worried about money, Vincent tried to kill himself to ease the financial burden. I think he was over-whelmed with guilt. His having been a minister suggested that he had a very active conscience at least. It was nothing new for genius to be allied to madness. He sounded terribly depen-dent, not only on Theo's money, but on his emotional support.

It seemed so unfair that Vincent had always been poor, paying seventy cents a day for a little cramped room in an attic. Toward the end of his life, he had painted seventy paint-ings and done several drawings too in a seventy-day period. At the going rate of upwards of fifty million per painting, he earned over three and a half billion dollars in a little more than two months. That must be more than Michael Jackson makes. And the poor devil died by his own hand, stony broke in a stifling attic. They laid his coffin on a billiard table, which sounded pathetic. There was a picture of his modest little head-stone in the cemetery at Auvers. Theo's was beside it just months later.

It seemed almost obscene that people were buying Van Gogh's pictures now for such wild sums of money. And that Latour and Bergma were exploiting him was even worse. There was a moral repugnance in it. Vincent was such a good, simple, idealistic man. I felt a new eagerness to catch the crooks in honor of his memory. Some few characters have that ability to reach out and touch our hearts. This was becoming more than a case; it was a crusade.

When John came to the apartment that afternoon, I was still reading. I hastily stuffed the book under the sofa and opened the door. I had got so carried away I hadn't even fixed my hair or put on any makeup.

"What's new?" I asked, after he had taken advantage of my lipstick-less lips.

"In the case, you mean? Well, for starters, Denise has an unlisted phone, so we didn't get into her apartment. Gino's looking into her address. A pretty dull morning."

"You might as well have spent it with me."

"You needed your beauty sleep. Oh oh, I better rephrase that. You said you were tired from staying up late studying—and of course dating other guys," he added with a dark look.

"Thank God my exams are all over," I said, and hastily offered coffee, before he reopened that particular can of worms. He followed me into the kitchen while I put on the kettle.

"Did Gino have any luck finding out if Hot Buns has an alibi for six-thirty the night before last?" I asked.

"The people at the hotel say she arrived early, before seven, to help Bergma. That makes it pretty tight. We didn't like to question her. She's one of the best leads we've got so far. I'll do some discreet quizzing tonight and see how things stand with her and Bergma."

I tried not to resent Denise as I filtered the coffee and took it into the living room. I thought about the case and said, "Has Gino learned anything from the bugs on Bergma's phones?"

"Nothing. The guy hasn't tried to get in touch with whoever called him, or vice versa. It's all business. Bergma hasn't been any place except to his own house and the museum, so they haven't met."

"You know where the partner *could* meet Bergma without arousing any suspicion is at the art show opening tonight. There'll be tons of people there. If Bergma hasn't been in touch with him, he must be getting very jumpy. We figure he killed Latour for Jan Bergma. They've got things to talk about. Like the paintings, and where they are, and how they're going to unload them."

"If they have them," John added doubtfully. "Bergma told the caller 'They're gone.' That doesn't sound as if the caller knew. *One* of them damned well knew, and was trying to con the other."

"Bergma's returning to the Netherlands in January. He's got to meet the guy before then and clear things up. I know if it were I, I'd go to the opening tonight."

John nodded, interested. "We'll watch and see if any of the customers make Bergma especially nervous. See if he goes off into any private corners with anyone. I'll take my Bic Pic along. Maybe Interpol will recognize the guy. I might recognize him myself."

"It'll be tricky using your lighter. There won't be any smoking allowed."

"I don't have to know that. In France they smoke their heads off nearly every place but in church. It's only in the States that you can't smoke."

"And Canada. They're becoming rabid here. My uncle tells me they'll soon be having smoke police in Toronto, and you know how he loves his stogies."

There was nothing much to be done, case-wise, so we played hookey in the afternoon and I showed John Montreal. Mount Royal, Place des Arts, Place Ville Marie, and Brother André's Shrine on the mountain left him blasé. What really impressed him was the subway, so clean and quiet and beautiful, with murals and assorted artwork at every stop. He also seemed to take considerable pleasure from the soignée women, whom I must admit do have a certain *je ne sais quoi*.

To make up for his seeing Denise and my getting stuck with Gino that night, he was taking me out for a gourmet dinner first. Gourmet dinners and opening nights are to me what a canvas and a box of pigments must have been to Van Gogh. They make me a little crazy with joy.

I vacillated between the chic new black pencil dress and a flame red little number with a sparkly top and bubble skirt worn to the McGill Christmas formal. John had already seen the black, so I chose the red. As I didn't have time to get to a hairdresser, I wore my hair up again. I love the big, dangling new earrings. For Christmas, Sherry gave me a pair I had been ogling all fall at Birks. They consisted of a cluster of rhinestones, weighing about four ounces each, that fell in a cascade of glitter two inches below the ear. All this glitz called for extravagant makeup. I felt very French and sophisticated when John picked me up. He, in his Savile Row suit, looked dashing and debonair enough to please Robin Leach.

John smiled appreciatively. "Am I back in Paris?" he asked. "The coeds didn't look like this when I was at college."

"I caused a few riots," I said modestly.

We went to the French seafood restaurant in the Queen Elizabeth Hotel. The bouillabaisse alone is worth the trip. Fat black clams and assorted shellfish and other sea critters make it a meal in itself, although we managed to do justice to a coq au vin and a bottle of sauterne as well. I was too well fed and pleased with the world to let Gino bother me when he joined us later in John's room.

Gino had been taking his Hugh Heffner pills and had made some pretense at a toilette for the occasion. He wore a nice tan camel's-hair coat, not his usual parka. The trousers of his blue polyester suit had a crease, and he wore a shirt and a tie. I think some color of socks other than yellow would have been an improvement, especially when his tie was red, but what the heck. The fumes of the sauterne were still with me, and I greeted him politely.

"You look great, Newman," he said, running his shifty little eyes up and down my body. "This is a real class lady you're lending me, John. Too bad she's such a beanpole, or I might decide to cut you out entirely. Heh heh."

John reminded me of a German shepherd, patronizing a smaller mongrel. He just grinned good-naturedly and said, "That'd learn me."

"Is there any of that Johnnie Walker left?" was Gino's next sally. "I need something to take the smell of that garlic off my breath. Ma uses about a cup of garlic in her spaghetti. She crushes it to get the oils out."

Mrs. Parelli's trick works very well. I could smell the fumes across the room. The Scotch didn't help a bit to hide it either. I insisted on sitting in the back seat for the trip to the museum. "You and John probably have things to talk about," I said magnanimously.

"You really got your lady trained," Gino said approvingly to John.

"Cassie knows her place," he grinned. "Where else would a backseat driver sit?" His baleful expression as he tried to avert his nose from Gino's breath told me he understood my ploy.

The elite of Montreal were swarming into the museum when we arrived. Montreal is one of the few cities where furs are not only ornamental but also useful. Even the men wear them. There was a lot of fur climbing the steps—mink, ocelot, wolf, a few leopards, and beaver, the latter mostly on the men. Once the furs were stashed, I ogled what the women wore beneath them. If I thought my red dress was going to rate a second look, I was mistaken. In the Christmas season, three-quarters of the women opted for red and rhinestones, or diamonds, depending on the bank balance. The men were all as carefully groomed as TV evangelists, with their blow-dried hair and expensive tailoring.

A tall, gray-haired man in formal black evening wear headed up the reception line. I recognized Mr. Dupuis, the manager of the museum, from the newspapers. My eyes did not linger long on Dupuis. The fantasy beside him, also in black, was straight out of a French film. Had they imported Alain Delon for the evening? The man was tall, with a glossy head of black hair and that pale skin that suggests poetry and perhaps decadence, rather than ill health. His eyes were black and lustrous, fringed with lashes an inch long.

I was so smitten with his beauty that it didn't register for a minute when he introduced himself as Mr. Bergma. When it finally sank in, I pictured him in his red and black and white house and thought it was the wrong setting for him. He should live on the boulevards of Paris. It should be perpetually spring, with the lime trees in bloom, scenting the air. If he insisted on having a house, Versailles would do. A man who looked like that deserved to be surrounded by mirrors, the better to see him from all angles.

His hand that held mine in warm embrace was also pale, with a masculine smattering of dark hair. An ornate gold ring with a green stone bedizened one finger. A glimmering wafer of gold watch peeped out from under his white shirtcuff. It came as no surprise that his accent was delightfully cosmopolitan, more French than anything else. It was a disappointment that he hardly glanced at me. His lustrous eyes were scanning the new arrivals. Perhaps for the man he had forbidden to call him?

I continued down the line and soon regrouped with John and Gino. "Wow!" was all I could think of to say. "Did you get a load of that Bergma!"

"As cool a cucumber as ever stepped out of the refrigerator," Gino said. "I wonder where he got that suit."

John gave a disparaging look. "Don't tell me you fell for that greaser."

To call Jan Bergma a greaser was like calling Catherine

Deneuve a bleached blonde. There may have been a daub of something on his hair, but it was hardly the paramount impression. John was just jealous, of course, so I raved on to reinforce this emotion. If I had to put up with Hot Buns, why should he get away with no more competition than Gino?

"Let me have the job of watching Jan," I begged. I called him Jan instead of Bergma to infuriate John.

"I'd better circulate and see if I can find Denise," he retaliated, and stomped off.

Gino and I, awash in a cloud of garlic oil, watched Bergma for a while. It was a night right out of my dreams. Everyone was there—even the premier of Quebec, with his beaky nose and glasses. There were lots of politicians, financiers, people from the performing arts—actors, singers, a famous ballet dancer in a dress much like my own, and a gaggle of anonymous society people. The pop of flashbulbs and whir of TV cameras told us the press was there.

"I should've sprung for a new jacket," Gino said, looking at Bergma. "That'll teach me to spend my hard-earned money on a dishwasher. Did I mention I got Ma a dishwasher for Christmas?"

"Three or four times, but don't let that stop you. Repetition is the mother of learning."

"It has four settings. I got gold, to match her red kitchen."

"That sounds—bright."

When Bergma moved away from the door, I took a sharp look to see who he was with. Since it was the Minister of Culture, I acquitted him of being a murderer and took the chance to have a look at the exhibit. It was gorgeous. I'd return later to study it more thoroughly, but enjoyed a quick glimpse of the various displays. The jewelry was whimsical, with birds and flowers and animals fashioned of gold and gem stones. Cartier had some intriguing jewelry and small sculpture, and of course Erté was handsomely exhibited. What a genius! His fashion designs were extravagantly lovely. The twenties lived again in those elongated ladies in sweeping robes. I wasn't mad about his new line of watches, but they were interesting.

"What do you figure the watches go for?" Gino asked.

"Over a thousand, I imagine."

"What suckers! This little beauty cost me twenty-five bucks."
He proudly displayed an ugly hunk of chrome with many insets
on the dial. "Never loses a minute."

Across the room, I spotted John and Denise examining a
painting. I was gratified to notice John was keeping a close
eye on me. He wore a pugnacious expression, but when he
caught me looking, he turned and beamed an oily smile at
Denise. Hot Buns was in white, a rather matronly and unat-
tractive affair with a long, boxy jacket that thoroughly hid her
charms. Maybe the museum didn't want her to look like a
hooker. From the neck up, she foiled them. The mane of red
hair was frizzed to a fare-thee-well, and her earrings were even
bigger and gaudier than mine. Waiters, decked out like nineteenth-century footmen for some unclear reason, carried around
trays of champagne and hors d'oeuvres. Gino speared us a
glass and a plate.

"What the hell. This is costing John a bundle. We might as
well get his money's worth," he said. He took a bite of one
of the hors d'oeuvres and gagged. I was afraid he was going
to spit it out on the floor. "What *is* this stuff?"

"Looks like a pâté to me."

"Yuck. It tastes like lard. I thought Angelina's was bad.
And look at all these high-class people gobbling it up." He
put it in a handkerchief and slid it in his pocket.

The Minister of Culture met up with some noteworthy folks
and abandoned Bergma. I came to attention to see what Bergma
did, now that he was free. He was busy greeting assorted
socialites, mostly female. The men didn't seem crazy about
him, but the women were fawning. No handshakes for them;
they pushed their powdered and rouged cheeks forward for a
kiss. I discovered, or imagined, that he was nervous. That was
the only thing I could come up with. I stuck close enough to
hear what was being said, and it was all perfectly innocent
stuff about how marvelous and fantastic and exquisite the exhibition was, and what a treasure they had in dear Jan. A few
mentioned Mrs. Searle's party and other holiday festivities to
which he was bid.

It all seemed like a waste of time, except for the pleasure
of watching Jan's matchless face and form. My eyes were glued
to him when he suddenly gave a leap like a wounded animal.

His head shot up, his body turned rigid, and his pale face suffered a sudden infusion of blood. I followed the line of his eyes and saw him staring at an Arab.

At least I think the man was an Arab. He wasn't dressed in a burnoose or anything, but his skin was swarthy and he had those impenetrable, black eyes, like Jan himself. His hair was black, combed straight back. He looked about fifty years old, stocky of figure. He was wearing an impeccably tailored dark suit, and on his arm hung a highly ornamental young lady. I had an impression he was glaring at Jan in a meaningful way. He turned his head, spoke to his partner, and they moved on.

My next interest was in the partner. I decided he had either robbed the cradle or was with his daughter. The shy, wilting violet air suggested a daughter on her best behavior. She too had that dusky skin and black eyes; her mane of hair was long and curled, but the color matched her partner's. The eyes had a slightly oriental cast though—maybe his wife was an Oriental. As to the rest of her, she was just plain sexy, beautiful. One of those dainty women who appeal to men's chivalrous instincts. Beside her, even Hot Buns would look like a Clydesdale. She wore a deep-blue clinging gown that reeked of Paris. I thought the blue-and-white stones around her neck would be the real McCoy. There'd be a sable or some expensive fur parked at the coat check.

"It wouldn't take a Don Juan to fall for that lady!" Gino exclaimed. Odd how he gave that illusion of slavering without actually drooling. "More curves than a corkscrew. I wouldn't mind snuggling up to that." Only his physical repulsiveness saved him from promiscuity, I fear.

My eyes flew back to Jan. He had more or less recovered. The pink in his face was receding. I found it significant that he purposely turned his head directly away from the newcomers. Agatha Christie used the tingling of her thumbs to alert her to mystery. With me, it was more like the gang from *Chorus Line* doing kicks in my stomach. I had to notify John. I caught his eyes and gave him a wildly imperative toss of my head. Hot Buns was by his side, but chatting to someone. He spoke to her and nonchalantly weaved his way to me. "What's up?"

"The old guy in the dark suit, the one with the siren in blue. I think he's our third man. Jan nearly croaked when he came in. He seems to fill all the requirements. He's an Arab; therefore he's probably floating in money. He's interested in art, since he's here. And he glared at Jan. Jan leapt when he saw him. What do you think? Can you work the Bic Pic on them?''

John studied the man as he mingled with the crowd. The Arab seemed to know an awful lot of people, but none of the ones I recognized from newspapers. It wasn't politicians or actors or singers he was talking to; therefore it must be the social set. And that suggested contacts in the world of high finance.

"Get a load of the lady!'' Gino said, a piece of advice that was hardly necessary.

"I wonder who she is,'' John said, eyeballing her with the keenest interest.

"Aren't two at a time enough for you?'' I snipped.

"More than enough. It just happens I enjoy a better rapport with women. I'll tell you later what I've learned from Denise.'' His hand went into his pocket and he drew out the lighter-camera, but there really was no excuse to use it in this room. There were signs plastered all over the entrance forbidding smoking.

"Better not use it here,'' I said. "He might just notice a flame being lit for no reason. We don't want to make him suspicious.''

"Here, use my pen,'' Gino said, and pulled out a ballpoint, one of the cheapest ever manufactured.

"Is that a camera too?'' I asked in a low voice.

"Are you nuts? It's a pen. I always use a lighter to heat up the ink when it doesn't work. Lots of people do. Here, I'll give you one of my cards, John, and you pretend you're trying to write something.'' The card said Joe's Quick Lube. Fast, Cheap, Good.

That was what they did, after first edging close to our third man and taking careful aim. Neither the man nor his partner was paying the least attention to us. The man was deep in conversation with other businesspeople, and the woman was ogling all the celebrities. She smiled prettily at the TV show host and the conductor of the local symphony orchestra. John took pictures of them both; then tried to scribble something on the card with Gino's pen, which still didn't work.

"Okay, we've found out what we came for," Gino said. "Can we split now?"

I looked at John. "Have you decided whether you're taking Denise home?"

"Not yet," John said. "We want to be around if Bergma's friend makes contact. The friend will have to be followed when he leaves."

"You're the only one with a car. We'll all go," I said.

He rubbed his chin. "The thing is, I think I can learn more from Denise if I can get another couple of glasses of champagne into her. You and Cassie better follow the Arab, Gino. Make sure Cassie gets home safe, huh?"

"Does Hot Buns have wheels, or will you be taking a cab?" I asked.

"I don't know. The subject hasn't come up. I'll call you tomorrow, Cassie."

"Sure," I said airily, and cast a sheep's eye at Jan Bergma in retaliation. He actually noticed me, and smiled. "See you tomorrow then," I said, and wafted toward Jan to join the carnivorous matrons gathered around him.

"Good evening," he smiled. Every tooth a pearl. "I don't believe I've had the pleasure, Miss—"

"Newman," I said, and took his hand.

"I didn't think you were one of the museum's volunteers. I wouldn't forget anyone so lovely."

I could feel myself glow. "Actually I've been wanting to join. I'm a student at McGill. I wasn't sure the museum would be interested in someone who doesn't live in the city all year."

"Summer is not the busy season. We have several students from McGill." He went on to name the crème de la crème, all women. I knew some of them to speak to, and claimed friendly intimacy with them all, so he'd think I was somebody too.

"I'll certainly be in touch after the holidays then," I said.

"Excellent. I may not be here myself. I'm just on sabbatical. I'll be leaving in January, but don't let that deter you. Mrs. Searle is in charge of the Volunteer Committee. I'll speak to her."

"Oh you're leaving!" I said with a moue. "Not too early in January, I hope?"

"My term expires the thirty-first of December. I plan to return very soon after. Just a little ski trip to the Laurentians first. Do you ski, Ms. Newman?"

"I love it. I may still be at Tremblant at the New Year myself. Where will you be staying?" Any tidbits might prove useful.

"With friends—the Mrs. Searle I mentioned earlier. They have a chalet there. Perhaps we'll meet on the slopes?"

"At the top of the Minute Mile," I said gaily, and left, as he was beginning to show signs of impatience. One of the matrons had clamped a prehensile hand on him and was tugging. I didn't want John to see him walk away from me.

"Oh Ms. Newman!" he called after me, nice and loud. "Perhaps I could get your phone number?"

"I'm in the book," I assured him, with a come hither look.

His smile was extremely dashing and flirtatious. "So am I," he said.

This was great! Not only was I showing John how attractive I was, but in case of necessity, I had an excuse to phone Jan and dig for information. Best of all, John was scowling like a gargoyle. I walked unconcernedly back to the Erté exhibition, where he soon joined me.

"You realize that guy's dangerous," he said through clenched teeth.

"That's probably part of his charm."

"I hope you haven't given him your phone number!"

"He asked me for it, but I just told him I'm in the book—like him."

"He's not in the book. He's unlisted. I wish you hadn't given your real name. Remember what happened to Latour."

That sent a little chill scuttling up my spine. I *was* in the book. "We know Jan didn't kill him," I pointed out.

"He probably gave the order. We know he's in it up to his bedroom eyes. You're staying with me tonight."

"Will this be a ménage à trois or à quatre? You forget I'm with Gino."

He gave me a look that would freeze fire. "I knew I should never have told you anything about this business. Now I can't take Hot Buns home. I'll get back to her now. And I don't want you to leave Gino's side."

I smiled enigmatically. I was glad to hear "Denise" had become "Hot Buns." She seemed less of a threat when he called her that. While John induced Denise to tank up on the cheap domestic champagne, Gino and I watched all our suspects. We could vouch that Jan and the Arab hadn't exchanged a word. The lady in blue had managed a few flirtatious words with him, but I imagine she mistook him for a movie star. And anyway, they said only a few words.

When the Arab and his partner went for their coats, Gino darted off to John for the keys.

"I'm going with you," John said.

I guess he was afraid Bergma would follow and kill me or perhaps subject me to a fate that he not so fondly imagined to be worse than death.

CHAPTER 9

Gino stood in front of the museum watching to see which way the Arab's car went while John and I flew to get his wheels. The car proved easy to follow. It was a chauffeur-driven white stretch Lincoln limousine. It didn't go far either, just down the street to the most exclusive hotel in the city, the Ritz Carlton. As the chauffeur helped the lady alight, I noticed she was swathed in a floating wolf coat I would die for. John drove on a few blocks till he found a place to park.

"The guy sure isn't trying to lay low," Gino said. He was in the back now, breathing garlic fumes over our shoulders. "The car'll be easy to check out. There's a place rents them downtown. That'll be better than questioning the chauffeur. No point tipping our hand. I'll put a man at the Ritz."

John sat silent a moment, thinking. "I'll take the Ritz, Gino," he said. "I've got to stay somewhere. Why not be on the spot?"

"Suit yourself," Gino replied, "but it'll cost you an arm, a leg, and both balls. Did that guy look familiar to you? Those dusky foreigners all look alike, but I think I've seen that guy before. Or maybe just a picture."

"Denise said he's Sheikh Rashid something or other, from one of the United Arab emirates. Oil money," John said.

"That's it!" Gino crowed. "His mug was all over the papers yesterday. He's here to buy up some apartment buildings. Those oil sheikhs have more bread than Christies has cookies.

82

Jeez, I could sure think of something more fun than buying buildings.''

"Did the papers say anything about the woman with him?" I asked.

Gino screwed his face up to aid memory. "Secretary, Ms. LeeChee nut or something like that. Whether she ever personally met a typewriter is a mute [*sic*] point. There was a picture of her, too, trying to look sexy and innocent at the same time—like you, Newman. The only difference is, she succeeded."

"In which category did I fail?"

"Both," he answered without hesitation.

"Cut to the quick. Better read another *Playboy*. Your charm is slipping."

"Just kidding. You know my humor, Newman."

"To know it is to hate it."

"He's in the right income bracket to be the buyer of the Van Goghs," John said. "Can you do a run on him and see if he's been to the Netherlands in the last year or so, Gino?"

"Can-do, Weiss. I'll run the girl too."

"Good, let's cover all bases. She could be in on it."

"I'm freezing my butt off," was Gino's next speech. "Since you're moving to the Ritz, let's go to your place, Weiss. We'll kill that Johnnie Walker while you pack. It's already badly wounded. You drink too much, you know that?"

"Especially when you're around," John agreed blandly.

While John stuffed his belongings into a set of luggage that would not disgrace the Ritz, we picked his brains to hear what else he'd learned from Denise.

"She's a regular soap opera heroine," he told us. "She got her job through a boyfriend who taught at the Beaux Arts. I didn't tip my hand by asking for a name, but when she said he was murdered this week, I figured I knew who she was talking about."

"So she was Latour's girlfriend. Imagine her partying already!" I huffed.

"She's been through with Latour for a long time. Once she laid her baby blues on Bergma, she forgot about Latour."

I emitted a long sigh and breathed, "Naturally."

John gave me a look that would sour cream. "She had a fling with Bergma, but that seems to be all over too. Selfish, she called him. A womanizer. Are you listening up, Cass?''

"To every word. She seems to know all the right people, by which I guess I mean wrong people, but does she have anything to do with the Van Gogh business? Did she mention the portrait Latour did of her?''

"I didn't like to ask. I doubt if she's in on the scam. I think she just happened to be socially involved with Latour and Bergma.''

"She's man's plaything," Gino decided. "Where'd she meet Latour?''

"They're neighbors.''

I nearly jumped from my seat. "You mean she lives right there, in his building?''

"Like I said, they're neighbors. She lives on the floor below. They met on the elevator.''

"Then she might have killed him!''

John didn't look convinced. "She was at the hotel with Bergma, arranging the party when he was murdered. My gut feeling is that she's all right. What her story *does* confirm is that Latour and Bergma were old friends. She met Bergma through Latour. Once she started going out with Bergma, he didn't want her seeing Latour—at all. A fiend of jealousy, she called him, but I imagine Bergma just didn't want to risk her learning anything about the Van Goghs.''

"Did she see Latour again?'' I asked.

"Only to nod to, according to her story.''

Gino gave a bah of disgust. "She's in a perfect position to know what was going on. If Bergma didn't blab to her, Latour probably did—in spite or bragging. She had a grudge against Bergma.''

"But not against Latour," I pointed out. "*She* left *him*, and *he's* the one who's dead.''

"And we know Hot Buns didn't off him," Gino agreed, "but a woman like that wouldn't have any trouble finding a new guy to do her dirty work for her. If that's the scenario, she's got Bergma right where she wants him, hasn't she? She's got the hot pix. She calls the shots.''

John gave a very doubtful look. "I don't like to brand myself as an MCP, but from her talk, I don't think Denise is a deep thinker. More gossip than conversation, if you know what I mean.''

"It's easy for smart people to act dumb. She bears watching," Gino insisted. *"Cherchez la femme."*

John's mind had moved on to the other *femme* now in the case, Sheikh Rashid's lady. "You won't forget to find out whatever you can about the sheikh's secretary too, will you, Gino?"

"She'll be an international harlot," he decided, apparently unconcerned at being recognized as a dyed-in-the-wool MCP. "A freeloader, tagging along for the ride. A good looker though."

In about fifteen minutes, Gino rose. "We'll be in touch tomorrow. Are you using your own name at the Ritz, Weiss? Or will I be calling for Sean Bradley, the name you used in Toronto last summer?"

"Not a bad idea," John said, tugging pensively at his ear. "A Texas oil man and a sheikh should have something in common. Yeah, I'll be Sean Bradley. Do you happen to know where I could pick up a Stetson, Cass?"

I shrugged. "Somewhere in Place Ville Marie probably."

"That's the underground shopping mile, where they take you to the cleaners," Gino added. "I gotta buzz. *Au revoir.*" In an uncharacteristic fit of gallantry, he performed a bow in my direction, thanked me for a lovely evening, and left, slamming the door behind him.

I tried to look irresistible because I had a plan to involve myself more deeply in the case and had a feeling John wasn't about to oblige me. "You're all set," I mentioned, looking at his luggage. "I guess it's time for us to go to my place while I throw a few things into a bag."

John looked alarmed. "You're not going home!"

"Home is where the heart is. Didn't you say it was too dangerous for me to be alone, with Jan knowing my address? You were going to stay with me. Well, you're going to the Ritz. Whither thou goest . . .''

"Oh jeez." John looked thoroughly frustrated. "We can't check in together. If your mother ever found out . . .''

I had fully impressed on John when we first met that my mother was of the old school. First marriage; then sex. All right, so nothing happened last night! John is a few years older than I—about a decade older actually. He seems to feel he would be taking advantage of a minor if he did more than kiss me. I fully appreciate his strength of character and gallantry; it's a refreshing change, but that is not to say I could allow it to get in the way of our case.

"How could she find out? She's in Maine. That handsome, murderous lecher Bergma, on the other hand, is right in Montreal, with my phone number in his pocket." I played my trump card and added, "Of course he won't be able to reach me if I'm not at my apartment. Maybe I better stay there."

John's mustache bristled. "You realize this is blackmail?"

"I would call it that, yes."

"How long will it take you to pack?"

"About five minutes. I already have my things set aside for going home. All I have to do is put them in a bag."

"Let's go then."

"You better see if they have a room at the Ritz first."

"Two rooms," he countered.

"Oh, a suite! Nice! You're an awful grouch, but you *do* travel first class."

"Two rooms," he glared. He went to the phone and ordered a suite for himself, and an adjoining room for his secretary. "If a sheikh can travel with his secretary, a Texas oilman can do the same," he said firmly.

We went down to the lobby, John checked out, left our forwarding address for Menard, and we went to my apartment, where I hastily gathered up what I thought I'd need for our stay. It wasn't till we were in the car that I remembered John's Christmas present, still under the sofa. While we drove to the Ritz, we discussed future plans.

"Tomorrow I'll ditch this car and hire us a limo," he said. I gurgled for joy. "Menard can drive for us. We'll need more than an ordinary chauffeur. He seemed like a bright enough guy."

"Do you plan to meet the sheikh or just be around to follow him?"

"Whatever. It won't be easy to strike up an acquaintance with a sheikh."

Knowing who he would get along better with, I quickly

claimed the lady in blue for my own. "Maybe I can meet his secretary. She must have time on her hands while he's out wheeling and dealing."

That pleased him. He thought I'd be safely and busily out of his way, and out of danger. I felt like a pampered darling when we pulled up in front of the canopy of the Ritz and a doorman in a great coat and cap hopped to open our door and assist me out. The Ritz is a small hotel, discreetly elegant rather than opulent. It's where people like the sheikh and Liz Taylor put up when in Montreal. The service was extremely gracious. A porter was summoned by a nod of the head to tote our bags. A bell would be too intrusive. Things don't ring at the Ritz. They hum.

I nearly swallowed my tongue when I recognized our porter, and worse, he recognized me. It was a classmate from the university, a black exchange student from Africa, who apparently worked there part time to subsidize his allowance. I didn't know his last name, but everyone on campus knew Export A. It was the style to call him "Export, eh?" Canadians have the verbal idiosyncracy of ending every second speech with "eh?" Export A was his middle name. His first one was hard to pronounce. He said he was named after a cigarette his dad's boss smoked. He had a younger brother called Atari.

Export A was a tall, very well built young man who wore a perpetual smile. He schooled his smile to polite proportions, pretending he didn't recognize me, when he saw me with John. I felt like two cents, realizing my reputation was being sluiced down the toilet. Then it occurred to me that Export A might be very helpful. An insider—he might know useful things about the sheikh.

Once we were safely installed in the elevator, I let him know he could recognize me. "Not going home for Christmas, Export?" I asked.

"Flying isn't cheap. You're staying too, huh?" he grinned. He arrived in Canada with an English accent and vocabulary, but had a quick ear for dialect. He watched a lot of TV, and within a month he began to sound like an American black.

"Yes, I'm working. This is my—boss, Mr. Bradley," I said. John nodded and smiled his innocent smile.

I waited till we were in our rooms before saying more. The

rooms were old-world, laidback elegant, which frankly is not my own first choice of elegance. If you've got it, flaunt it. I have nothing against the modern luxury of whirlpool baths and duvets and deep-pile carpets, even if they're not Persian. I had a whispered colloquy with John, while Export A arranged the luggage and drew the drapes and things, and got his permission to ask my friend's help.

"Have you got a minute to spare, Export?" I asked.

He gave a deep, mock bow, and a grin that lit up the whole room. "I'm here to serve, Ma'am."

"Do you, by any chance, serve Sheikh Rashid and his secretary?"

"Do I? Man, we have knock-down-and-drag-out fights for the honor. That dude tips twenties."

"What rooms are they in?"

"Right below you—the royal suite," he said, and quoted the price per diem, which was staggering.

"How long have they been here?" John asked.

"Arrived Sunday, three days ago, in a stretch limo big enough to hold a pool table. They say he flew in on his own Lear jet. I wouldn't know, but I don't have any reason to doubt it."

"Have they had callers?"

"Oh yeah, the sheikh has full-time dibs on the executive boardroom. He has lots of meetings. Goes out a lot too."

"What about his secretary?" I asked eagerly.

"Ms. Hejaz? She's a buy-till-you-die lady. One of the rooms is chockful of her bags and boxes. Man, she had sixteen pairs of shoes delivered yesterday. I didn't realize secretaries were so well paid! We figure the sheikh must give her ten grand of pin money a day. When she's not out buying, she has the stores bring stuff here for her to look at. That's about all she does— buy and eat and drink. Champagne with whipped cream on top." He screwed up his face in distaste. I thought it sounded lovely.

"Where is she from?" John asked.

Export A shrugged. "Citizen of the world, I guess. Oh yeah, one more thing. Ms. Hejaz is into tarot. She has a session every morning in her room with Madame Feydeau, a local fortune-teller. Some of the girls who work here know her. They say she's good, if you believe that kind of stuff. Ayesha—that's Ms. Hejaz—told the room maid that Madame is a high mistress of tarot. I bet Madame is lining her pockets real good."

John seemed uninterested in this line, although I saw a possibility of striking up an acquaintance with Ms. Hejaz. I didn't personally own a set of tarot cards, but I'd had a few amateur sessions in the coffee shop at the university. Or at least I could hire Madame and pick her brains.

"Would you happen to know, or could you find out, where the sheikh was at six-thirty the night before last?" John asked.

Export A looked suspicious. "What's going down here, folks? Do I smell cop?"

John hesitated a moment, and decided to take Export A fully into his confidence. He explained who he was, and why he was interested.

Export A was incensed. "The dude that sliced off his ear? Oh man, that's bad. I like Vincent van Gogh. My momma had his *Sunflowers* in her kitchen at home. Not the original," he added, rather unnecessarily. "But I don't think the sheikh did it. I'll double-check, but I seem to recall he had a meeting all that afternoon. Went on till seven-thirty or eight. Yeah, that's right. I didn't work Monday. I studied all day for Psych One, and came in Tuesday at three. All the staff were talking about the big tips floating around. We all wanted to get to serve the boardroom dudes. They had sandwiches sent in at six, and worked till eight. Then the sheikh and Ms. Hejaz ate in the hotel dining room at about nine."

"You're sure about that?" John asked.

"Sure as bees make honey, Sir. But last night he and Ms. Hejaz ate out. They left at six-thirty. Had reservations at Le Jardin restaurant, and tickets for the symphony."

"Last night's no good," John said. "It's the night before we're interested in." John slid a bill into Export A's fingers and said, "There's lots more where this came from if you keep us informed."

I judged by Export A's smile that the bill was of a substantial denomination. "Yes, Sir!" He left, and John began pacing.

"A boardroom full of witnesses. It looks like we can strike the sheikh off our list of suspects," he said. "You're sure we can trust Export A?"

"What reason would he have to lie? He's just a student."

"He should be okay. Lucky you know him. This won't do your reputation at school any good, will it, being shacked up at a hotel with a man?"

"I'm a ruined woman," I smiled. "A good thing I'm wearing red. The *A* on my dress won't show up."

"I wouldn't want your classmates getting the idea you do this often."

"For heaven's sake, John, they're not nuns. My roommate seldom sleeps at home on weekends."

"What! You mean you're there *alone*. You *are* alone?"

"Just me and my telephone, which sometimes doesn't ring for weeks at a time."

It rang then, while I was speaking. "Gotta be Gino," John said, and picked it up. I listened while he told Gino what Export A had told us.

"He'll call again in the morning," John said when he hung up. "Now you and I better get some shut-eye."

I heard him lock the adjoining door behind me. He hadn't even kissed me goodnight. He was either still angry about my dating, or I was so irresistible he was afraid if he kissed me, he wouldn't be able to stop.

"Make sure your door's locked," he called through the door.

"You just took care of that, didn't you?"

"I mean your door to the hall."

"Say goodnight, John."

"Sleep tight."

CHAPTER 10

There was a message for me at the desk next morning from Export A, saying he came on duty at three in the afternoon, but if I wanted to speak to a waiter named Ronald Stack, he could be trusted. John didn't like the name Ronald, and nixed that idea. The note also said that the sheikh and Ms. Hejaz had ordered breakfast in their room at nine-thirty. That left me time to dash off to a book store after breakfast and pick up a set of tarot cards and a book explaining the mysteries of the procedure. John suggested I read it in the breakfast parlor with a view of the lobby so I could follow Ayesha if she left. I'd take my coat with me in case I had to follow her outside.

"What will you be doing?" I inquired suspiciously.

"Hiring our limo, and seeing if Gino has learned anything. He's supposed to call. He's got a man set to follow the sheikh if he leaves. I want to know if Bergma and the sheikh meet. I also want to see who they talk to. Since neither of them personally plunged the knife into Latour's back, one of them hired someone to do it."

"What about Hot Buns?" I asked.

"We'll have to go over her apartment too."

"Gino thinks she's a good suspect."

"I wonder if that could be because she thinks he's a creep. You wouldn't believe the crude line he used on her."

"Wouldn't I? What makes you think he didn't try it on me?"

"He hit on you! The bastard." He was more amused than concerned.

"Not to worry, John. He's so short, he only hit my ankle."

"If I hear of him buying a ladder, I'll take care of him."

"What time will you be back?"

"For lunch, I hope. Take care."

He left, and I immersed myself in the extremely complicated business of learning tarot. What I had was a book on the Rider–Waite method. There are seventy-eight cards in the deck, for crying out loud. It was suggested the student sleep with them under his or her pillow for five days to set up the proper vibes. That advice had to be ignored, along with the bothersome suggestion of keeping the cards under lock and key. I struggled with Major Arcana and Minor Arcana, and finally discovered there's a shortcut. Although my book said the full deck should be used, it was possible to give a reading using only the Major Arcana, with a manageable twenty-two cards. The cards were enormous, incidentally, and very pretty, with all sorts of symbols as well as the pictures.

I was still hard at it when a rather bizarre-looking lady arrived. She was about six feet with hair dyed jet black, which looked strange around her withered, painted face. I figured any lady wearing a turban with a frizz of black hair below it and decked out in an embroidered cloak had to be into the occult. By loitering around the desk, I heard the clerk call her Madame Feydeau. About five minutes later, the sheikh came down and got into his white limo. I knew he was being followed, so I went back to my cards and my umpteenth cup of coffee. In a place like the Ritz, they don't give you dirty looks for lingering an hour over your coffee.

The tarot session with Ms. Hejaz lasted three-quarters of an hour. I ordered yet another cup of coffee and waited to see if Ms. Hejaz hit the bricks for her daily shopping spree. She did, wearing the wolf coat, and by luck, she didn't take a cab either. I followed behind her and spent a very boring morning waiting around outside the most exclusive shops in Montreal. After she had emptied the shelves of Gucci, she strolled along to Benetton's. Ms. Hejaz always came out empty-handed, but I knew that only meant her goodies were being delivered.

This was beginning to be not only a bore, but a dreadful

waste of time. The only thing even slightly unusual that she did was to make a phone call from Murray's Restaurant, where she stopped for lunch. Murray's was a family restaurant, not her style at all. Was I ever glad to get in out of the cold! She paid absolutely no attention whatsoever to me, so I felt I could safely follow her in. The lunchtime crowd offered good cover. Her phone conversation was brief. I figured she was calling the sheikh to let him know she was eating out. Not that it matters, but she ate only a salad. I also phoned the hotel and left word for Mr. Sean Bradley that I was eating out.

When Ms. Hejaz started shopping again in the afternoon, I went back to the hotel. A red-faced John was pacing the floor of his room, tearing his hair.

"Where were you?" he hollered. "I didn't know what had happened to you when I got that message!"

"I told you, I was eating out. I was following Ms. Hejaz. Boy, talk about shop till you drop! She makes Ms. Marcos look like an amateur. What did you do?"

He begin to simmer down. "Don't scare me like that, okay? We frisked Denise's place. It was clean. I got the limo. Gino says Rashid went to a real-estate agent downtown. A platoon of briefcases and the sheikh went to a high rise and spent the morning tapping walls and whatnot. It seems he really is buying the building."

"Tell me about Denise's apartment. What's it like?"

A telltale flush colored his neck. "Just an ordinary apartment," he said vaguely.

"She was there, wasn't she, John?"

"Of course not! She was at work."

"Then why are you blushing?"

"Blushing!" The blush deepened to beet.

"You didn't happen to drop in at the museum, by any chance?"

"I spoke to Denise," he admitted, attempting an air of non-chalance. "Didn't learn much. Bergma seems to be carrying on business as usual. He's going on a ski trip in the Laurentians before he leaves the country."

"I could have told you that. He'll be staying at Mrs. Searle's ski lodge."

"Where's that?"

"Someplace in the Laurentians. Will we have to follow him?" I asked hopefully. "Jan and I sort of have a date to meet at the top of the Minute Mile."

He gave me another of his cream-curdling looks. "There's one thing we might check out," I said. "Ayesha made a phone call at lunch. When Export A comes in, I'll have him find out if she called here, leaving a message for the sheikh."

"What we've got to do is find the paintings. They're not at Bergma's or Denise's place. If the sheikh has them, they could be in his room, maybe in one of those boxes Ms. Hejaz is storing up."

"Export A might be able to sneak us in."

At two-thirty, before he went on duty, Export A tapped at the door. "Hi, folks. What's shaking?" he asked.

"How's chances of getting us into the sheikh's room for a quick search?" I asked.

He looked very doubtful. "Man, that could cost me my job. Maybe my visa if the hotel found out and reported me."

"You're right," John said. "Too risky." Still, I thought the gentlemen exchanged a somewhat conniving look. It might be arranged at some time Export A knew for sure they were gone for a few hours. Right now, we didn't know when they were expected back.

I asked him to check the switchboard. Ms. Hejaz hadn't called, but that didn't mean much. She might have been calling any of the stores she visited.

"The parcels are beginning to arrive," Export A said. "Skis, snowsuit, stuff like that."

John and I exchanged a startled look at this coincidence. Bergma was going skiing too. John dashed to the phone and called Gino. He wasn't in, but he called back shortly after Export A left, and John asked him to find out exactly where Mrs. Searle's ski lodge was. The wilds of ski country might provide a fine and private place for their business.

"Maybe we should shop for skis too," I said.

"We'll rent them. Do you ski?"

"I'm from Maine, remember? Of course I ski—badly, but I ski."

"Actually we have some shopping to do ourselves. You mentioned Place Marie, where I might pick up a Stetson." He looked at my gray wool slacks and added, "You could use a few glad rags too, Cass. We've got to keep up with the Sheikh Jones's."

I imagine my face glowed like a Christmas tree. Visions of fur coats and diamonds danced in my head. But that was too much. I'm esurient, but I'm not without principles. I couldn't take furs and jewelry, not even from John. "You can rent furs," I said. "And who can tell paste jewelry at a glance?"

We had a perfectly delightful afternoon. Export A was paid to tell us what went on back at the hotel. John and I went on a shopping spree that challenged Ms.Hejaz's. I liked my rented ocelot coat better than her wolf. It had a big swaying back as full as a blanket and ten times as warm. My "jewels" were only imitations, but very good ones, and very expensive too. John enjoyed spoiling me as much as I enjoyed being spoiled. I exhorted regularly that he was spending too much money. I didn't need *two* cocktail dresses, although I was glad I didn't have to make a choice between the white and the gold lamé. One cashmere sweater would have been enough. Two was extravagant, and the third, a lovely mauve pullover, was downright decadent. I firmly forbid him to buy the most expensive of them all, a white turtleneck.

"They can be Christmas presents," he said, the dear uxorious man.

"Some token!" I cringed to think of that measly Van Gogh book, gathering dust under the sofa.

"Don't feel bad. They're all deductible. Maybe the company will spring for them. If we crack this case, we'll *buy* you the coat."

"First marriage; then furs and sex."

I received some very envious looks from the saleswomen when John tipped his white Stetson and called me darlin', in his phony Texas drawl. I think he had a good time too. Christmas would be an anticlimax after this afternoon. Winning a lottery would hardly outdo it. We're talking heaven here. We finally drove back to the hotel, and Menard toted our parcels up to our suite. Not only the back seat but the trunk too of the Caddie (unstretched) was full to overflowing, and Caddies have big trunks. Export A called before I had time to take things out of their packages and admire them some more.

"Your friends have just gone into the bar. Thought you might like to know," he said. "We can't do their rooms now, but you might overhear something if you feel inclined to have a cocktail."

I hung up. "How would you like a drink, John?" I asked, and gave Export A's message.

I made a quick change into my new mauve cashmere sweater and white flannel slacks. John suggested some glittery jewelry. I explained sparkling jewels and slacks didn't hit it off, but we compromised on a little fake diamond pin in the shape of a treble clef pinned to my sweater.

Ms. Hejaz looked bored and beautiful and still slender in a bulky white Irish string sweater. Her jet hair was arranged in careful abandon around her face and shoulders. The only jewelry she wore was an emerald the size of a grape on her right hand. We got a seat as close as possible to them. The bar was crowded, and we sat at one of two tables vacant, so it didn't look suspicious. She wasn't drinking champagne with whipped cream. What she held was a glass of clear, colorless liquid. The sheikh was having a Scotch on the rocks.

They hardly spoke at all. I read in something of Balzac's that "In a couple, there is always one who suffers and the other who is bored." I don't like to disagree with a genius, but it looked to me as if they were both bored to tears, though not otherwise suffering. When Rashid finally broke the silence, we were presented with a new problem. We hadn't counted on their speaking Arabic, which they were. At least I assume it was Arabic. It wasn't any language either John or I recognized.

John gave a defeated look. "They understand English," I said, *sotto voce*. "Maybe if we talk about something they're interested in, like oil or tarot, they'll start talking to us. They certainly look bored to flinders with each other."

I looked at John and said, "I wish I could arrange a reading. I'm really worried about your merger, John. We should have a tarot session before you decide."

John squirmed uncomfortably, perhaps not wanting the sheikh to think he put any faith in such things. "The hotel might be able to put you on to someone," he said.

"I don't want just anyone. There are so many phonies around. That woman in New York—I'm sure she didn't know what she was doing. She dealt the cards from the right.''

"Really?"

"And she didn't concentrate while she was shuffling and preparing the spread. She gabbed all the time, and just flung the cards on the table, without spacing them. Her aura was very poor. I don't trust her. Besides, she said you aren't good for me," I said, gazing dreamily at him and holding his hand. I felt Ayesha's black head turn in my direction. She didn't say anything, but I had caught her interest. Or John had. That was always a horrendous possibility. He was ten times as handsome as Sheikh Rashid.

"I think I better call Texas," John said, and lifted his hand for a phone.

He kept the button pushed down and pretended to make a call. He did a bit of loud talking about the price per barrel and capping his wells if that's all he was offered. The sheikh didn't move a muscle. He looked perfectly impassive, like a Buddha. He ordered another Scotch, and Ayesha settled for a Perrier, which seemed a strange restraint for a lady who takes whipped cream in her champagne. The waiter looked very impressed with his tip.

They left soon after. Pretty as Ayesha was, I noticed she was rather broader in the beam than I had thought, or than was desirable in a mistress. The woman had no self-control. Her spending showed that. The desk clerk met the sheikh at the door and gave him a message. Ayesha looked back at us, and on an impulse, came to our table.

She smiled rather shyly and spoke with a trace of an English accent, which surprised me. "I couldn't help overhearing you just now," she said. "If you're looking for a good tarot reader, I can give you a lady's phone number. Madame Feydeau. I have her card here somewhere."

She drew out the card. I thanked her effusively and wrote the number down. Madame Feydeau was of very limited use to me. I wanted to cement a bond with Ayesha and said, "It's so fascinating, isn't it? I'm studying the art myself. My last teacher felt I had the gift."

"Really? That's wonderful."

Then she looked nervously toward the sheikh and darted off before we could introduce ourselves. He was glaring, as he

had glared at Bergma at the museum. But I had made contact.
I could speak to Ayesha next time Export A alerted me she
was in the coffee shop or bar. In fact, I could even "lose"
Madame Feydeau's phone number.

John, the incurable romantic, had noticed Rashid's glare and
come up with a novel idea. "I begin to wonder if Ayesha is
traveling with him by choice, or compulsion," he said.

"A lady in distress for you to rescue?" I asked. "She did
seem a little nervous, but if he's a tyrant, he's a generous one.
I bet she spends ten thousand a day. I see why he hires a stretch
limo. John!" A new idea had assaulted me, and I sort of
shrieked his name.

"Sean," he reminded me in a low voice.

"The limo! He could have the pictures in the trunk!"

"By God, you're right!"

We dashed straight up to our rooms and John left a message
for Menard to call him. While we waited, he said, "Rashid
didn't use the little brass knife himself, and I doubt if he'd
send his hit man in such a noticeable car, but the trunk would
make a damned good hiding place."

"Yes, and I've just had another brainwave."

"I should take you out drinking more often."

"What I'm thinking is, you hired Menard to play chauffeur.
Who's to say Rashid doesn't travel with a hired assassin, a
general man of all dirty work? Can Menard find out who his
driver is?"

John was excited at the possibility. "Gino could do it easier." He started making phone calls. For the next half hour he
played telephone Ping-Pong with Menard and Gino. When
Gino called back, the conversation seemed to dull John's interest. "Oh, hired the chauffeur here, huh? It's still possible
he brought a henchman along with him. Can you get on to
customs and find out? There's got to be a third man. Yeah,
we'll be here till dinnertime I guess."

He hung up. "The chauffeur was hired locally. You don't
trust a stranger in dirty business like this. It seems kind of
funny Rashid doesn't have a real secretary along, now that I
think of it. The kind of business he's transacting, he should
have a whole phalanx of lawyers and accountants."

"He took a batch to look at the apartment building with him."

"All local. Of course he'd need lawyers who know the Canadian laws for buying in Canada."

"He's probably not interested in that building at all. It's just an excuse to come to Montreal and steal the pictures," I suggested.

"It's a damned awkward way of doing business. If stealing the pictures was to cut out Bergma, as well as Latour, why not handle Bergma after he makes the exchange at the museum in Amsterdam? When a case gets too complicated, I always wonder if I'm not on the wrong track. This one's got more twists than the Paris subway."

"Could Bergma have convinced Rashid that the forgeries are the originals?" I ventured.

"They weren't even aged yet. Some of Van Gogh's paintings are quite badly faded. The ones we saw looked brand new. The paint on the last one was still a bit soft. No, what makes good, simple sense is that Bergma meant to age them and substitute them when he returns to Amsterdam."

We thought and talked a little more. "Maybe it's time to rattle Bergma's cage a little," John said. "I could call him and make some threatening mention of the slides and notes I took from his house. That might nudge him into calling his partner at least, and we'd find out who the third man is."

"Or woman," I added, thinking of Hot Buns.

Menard had no success with getting into the trunk of the Lincoln limo, and John told him to forget it. He'd have Gino handle it. He called Gino and arranged it. Export A called at five and told us the sheikh and Ms. Hejaz were going to a Christmas performance of the *Nutcracker Suite* at the Place des Arts. "Should be out of their rooms for several hours," he added meaningfully. "Will it be convenient for me to call on you folks at eight-thirty?"

"That'll be just fine, Export." I smiled, hung up, and told John.

"Good. Gino should call before then. If the paintings are in the trunk of the limo, we won't have to bother your friend. What do you figure I should pay him for this?"

"I think we're talking a C note here, John."

He gave a weird look. "What have you been reading?"

"I don't read. I'm a scholar. I watch the late shows on TV."

"When you're not out dating other men."

Gino called back before our discussion degenerated into an argument. The pictures weren't in the trunk of the limo, so the search was on.

CHAPTER 11

Curious to see how Ayesha dressed for an evening at the ballet, I went down to the lobby at eight-fifteen on the pretext of buying a newspaper. The wolf coat hid most of what she had on, but diamonds glittered at her ears and throat, and a bit of something red and chiffony showed when she walked. She looked right through me, as if she'd never seen me before. I may not possess one of the world's fabulous faces, but was I that forgettable? She didn't look happy or as if she was looking forward to her glamorous evening at all. I began to wonder if John was right, and the sheikh was holding her in some diamond and velvet prison. Was she afraid to speak to me?

It's easy to despise a woman like Ayesha, who is living high off the hog without working. In my deepest heart, I did despise her, yet if that was the life she had freely chosen, why was she so—unexcited with her success? I can't use the word unhappy. She didn't look unhappy. She didn't look anything, except bored. Or maybe just a tinge frightened?

I had no conception of how a woman became what she was. I didn't even know her nationality. Perhaps she was one of those pitiable third-world girls, sold into white slavery while still a veritable child. You read of horror stories like that from time to time. Maybe she didn't realize there was a different kind of life open to her. I determined that I'd get through to Ayesha, and I was beginning to realize that it would have to be done when the sheikh was busy elsewhere. He usually had business meetings in the morning. Tomorrow morning I'd phone her, and try to ingratiate myself. She must be lonesome. Surely she'd welcome the chance to make a friend. Her superficially glamorous life must be a kind of hell really, with only that taciturn, sullen sheikh for company. And who knew what freakish sexual practices he inflicted on her?

I bought a copy of the *Gazette* and went back upstairs. Export A came to the door a little later, while John and I were looking through the paper. I could tell Export A's nerves were jangling. He kept wiping his palms on his trouser legs, and moistening his lips.

"We'll go down on the elevator together and see if the coast is clear," he said. "The suite next door is empty, so it's just the rooms across the hall we have to worry about."

The hall was empty. We scuttled along and Export A let us in. The rooms were even fancier than ours, and quite a bit larger. The dull gleam of well-polished mahogany and glint of brass set the tone. Underfoot, Persian carpets had faded to dignified middle age.

"She keeps the parcels in there," Export A said, tossing his head toward the adjoining door.

"You check her boxes and bags, Cass," John said. "I'm going to have a quick look through his briefcase."

We were all on edge, as though we were robbing a bank or something. I didn't know just how influential the sheikh was, but a powerful man like that could probably make it very hot for us if we were caught. A quick glance showed us the living arrangements were the same as John's and mine: a bedroom for Ayesha, a sitting room that the sheikh appeared to be using for an office, and his bedroom next to it. Export A kept his eye glued to the peephole while John and I rifled.

The first surprise was that there wasn't a single bag or box in her bedroom, or anywhere else. She had already packed her purchases then, and the servants had taken away the wrappings. I was looking for luggage, I figured, and found mountains of it in the closet. A matched set of Vuitton that looked brand new but had plenty of airport tags on the handles. That must have cost the sheikh several thousands. I took the bags to the bed, one by one, and soon learned there were no canvases in them. What there was was enough clothes to last a whole family a lifetime. Everything—fancy handstitched silk lingerie, sweaters, blouses, slacks, suits, gowns, bikinis, scarves, gloves. There was another fur coat hanging in the closet. The sable had a Paris label.

I took a quick look under the bed, on closet shelves, and in the desk and dresser drawers. No pix, just a copy of the *National Enquirer* and a bunch of movie magazines, which was rather pathetic. In the top dresser drawer there was a not so little velvet traveling case full of assorted bijoux that should have been in the hotel safe.

I went into the next room and called to John in a loud whisper, "She's clean. How are you doing?"

I saw he was examining passports, and went to have a look at them. "They're the most peripatetic pair since what's his name went around the world in eighty days. Look at this— Saudi Arabia, Jordan, Turkey, all across Europe and the States."

They, or at least Ayesha, reminded me more of that bird that could never land, because it had no feet. Huma, was it? Something small and vulnerable.

John's finger pointed to one stamp. Netherlands, it said. They'd been there thirteen months ago, both of them. I was a little surprised they'd been together that long.

"Just the right time for them to have met with Bergma and arranged the deal," he said. "He left Amsterdam a year ago. It looks like more than a coincidence they were there just before Bergma left, and arrived here in Montreal just before he goes home. The logical thing would be for Rashid to meet him in Amsterdam. Why did he come here, if not to grab the pictures?"

"It looks suspicious all right," I admitted.

John glanced at a pile of papers on the desk. "He really is buying the office tower," he said. "For sixty-five million cash. You have to wonder why a guy that rich would diddle Bergma out of his pay."

"Maybe that's how Rashid got so rich."

"No, it's oil money. Bergma can't be charging him anything near what those paintings would bring on the open market. I'd be surprised if he's getting more than a couple of million for the lot. That'd be chicken feed for Rashid. It just doesn't add up.''

Export A called softly over his shoulder, "You guys nearly done? I can't stay here all night. I have duties downstairs.''

"All done," John said, and we slipped out the door.

There was no one else in the elevator. I mentioned all the movie magazines. "I think she's another airhead, like Denise," I said.

Export A laughed. "Ms. Hejaz is an actress, or was, in the kind of movie where the women don't wear any clothes, if you know what I mean.''

"How do you know that?" I demanded.

"One of the guys recognized her. Tommie's into erotica. He rents all the blue movies. That's why Ms. Hejaz is always asking if any movie stars have checked in. She wants to get into legit movies. She is one real celebrity hunter. We get twenty bucks if we call her when any movie stars are checking in.''

"She certainly has the looks," I admitted. But she didn't have the personality. She was shy. It must have been painfully degrading for her to have to take off her clothes and perform in front of the moviemakers. She was probably exploited by other men before she met up with Rashid. After that, he'd seem like a savior.

Export A said, "She better lay off the champagne and whipped cream. That ass isn't getting any smaller." I wanted to strike him.

John slid a wad of bills into Export A's fingers as we left the elevator and said, "Thanks, Export. Keep up the good work.''

We went back to our room. "Poor Ayesha," I said sadly. "I bet she's just some poor, ignorant kid that fell in with the wrong company.''

"She doesn't have a 'poor kid' accent. Sounded like Mayfair to me.''

"Whoever put her into blue movies probably gave her speech lessons.''

John listened, and considered this possibility. "If she's as innocent as we think, we'll try to give her a helping hand when the sheikh's busted.''

"Would you, John?"

"*We*—we'll help her."

In all the excitement, we had forgotten about dinner. I didn't like to be eternally suggesting food, but I'd only had a sandwich for lunch. Before I had to mention my growling stomach, he asked, "Where would you like to eat? The dining room downstairs is good, and it'll be easy for Gino to find us."

I was just looking over my new wardrobe when Gino called. John peeped his head in and said, "Gino wants to meet us. How does the Trattoria grab you?"

"Italian's fine." But the Trattoria was not fine enough to merit a gown. I wore the navy cashmere sweater and gray pinstripe flannels. Thinking of John, I pinned on the rhinestone treble clef sign, and thought of my uncle. I'd have to phone Uncle Victor and wish him a Merry Christmas.

I kept thinking of Ayesha. If we were in Toronto, my uncle could introduce her to some TV or movie producers. Victor knew all the arty people. A lot of movies, even big American movies, were being shot in Toronto. Maybe if she could get started on a real career, she could straighten out her life. It was hard to tell her age, but she was still plenty young and lovely enough to make a career in acting. With her exotic appearance, she could represent half a dozen countries. If I could arrange it, it would be my good deed for the year. A person who has so much should be generous. Although I was poor as a church mouse at the moment, I really had everything that mattered. I guess I was still haunted by Van Gogh's unnecessary suicide. No one had reached out a hand to help him, and the world had lost one of its geniuses at an early age. Vincent was beyond help, but I'd do it in his honor.

These thoughts receded to the bottom of my mind when I put on my rented ocelot coat and swooshed down to the waiting Caddie limo, to be driven to the restaurant.

Gino was deep into a plate of spaghetti by the time we arrived. How one man could make such a shambles of a table was a mystery. It looked as if he had assaulted a loaf of crusty bread and pounded it to smithereens. The whole table top was littered with crumbs, liberally sprinkled with splashes of tomato sauce.

He gave a look of surprise and ran his beady eyes from my

head to my toes when we met him. His next assault was on the Queen's English and good taste. "Are you wearing anything under that pelt, Newman, or are you starkers?"

"Dream on," I said, and removed the coat.

Gino turned to John. "Santie Claus came early this year. You sprung for a fur, huh? This is beginning to look serious. Next she'll be after you for a diamond to go with it."

John said, "How's it going, Gino?" and I, with great restraint, said nothing. What can you expect from a man whose only vehicle of culture is *Playboy*?

I studied the menu while they talked. Did I want linguine with clam sauce or chicken cacciatore? I wanted both, and a loaf of that bread that crumbled so divinely. I wanted a salad as big as Mom's soup tureen—oh, and minestrone! The mind boggled at such a plethora of choices. I settled for good food instead of chic and had the chicken cacciatore, while still listening to the men.

"I don't suppose you've had time to check out if the sheikh brought a man or men along with him?" John asked.

"I did, and it wasn't easy, Weiss. You'd think Rashid was a head of state or something."

"He is, in a way."

"He's not the big cheese in his country, just a lesser sheikh. His dad was top man. Rashid was ousted. He took a couple of billion dollars and avoided a bloody coup. He's done bugger-all for his country. He's one of the international jet set playboys."

John listened politely. "But did he bring any men with him?"

"He has his own pilot. The guy's a Yankee, just hired last month. He was laid off one of the big airlines for what they called ill health. Probably either drugs or booze, but he has no record. The guy's over sixty. He has a terrific pension. I doubt if he'd suddenly take up a life of crime. Anyway he took straight off for the ski slopes after they landed." John and I exchanged a look. "Before Latour was knocked off," Gino added.

"I was thinking more on the lines of a business associate," John said.

"The sheikh travels alone, except for his so-called secretary. Oh I found out something about the tart. She used to make porno movies."

I glared. John said, "Yes, we heard about that."

"Get any titles?" Gino asked, with a lecherous light in his eyes.

"No, but I did learn something else interesting." He told Gino about the passports, and the sheikh's being in the Netherlands last year.

"If we needed a clincher, that's it," Gino said. "It all comes down to figuring out who actually killed Latour. Not Bergma, not Rashid, and probably not Ms. Painchaud. Her alibi isn't cast iron, but she's only a woman." I glared again; Gino grinned, knowing he was getting to me. "Rashid's never been in Canada before, and he wouldn't trust a stranger. It must be a friend of Bergma's we're looking for. Whoever he is, he's gone into deep hiding. Not a phone call, not a visit, nothing. Zip."

"And whoever did it must be holding the paintings," John added.

"Right," Gino said. "That's all you're really interested in. How much will you make if you find them and block that claim, Weiss? A million bucks, something like that?"

John just laughed and shook his head. "Rumors of our bonuses are greatly exaggerated."

"Sure, and that pelt Ms. Newman's wearing is bought on the installment plan."

"It's rented, actually," John told him.

"When guys start talking down how much dough they've got, I know they're loaded. How much do you figger Bergma will get for the pix?"

"Probably a couple of million."

"And they say crime doesn't pay."

"It's the worst bargain since Esau sold his birthright for a mess of pottage," John said.

Gino blinked. "Who?"

"Esau, in the Bible. Don't you read the Bible?"

"No, I'm a Catholic. Who'd he sell it to?"

John frowned. "Jacob," I told him. "And the pottage was lentil soup."

"No kiddin'. You're a mine of useless information, Newman. That what they teach you at McGill?"

"That, and how to use a knife and fork," I retaliated.

"I know all about manners. It's just these tables—they're too close together. They got us sitting bumper to bumper. Or do I mean bum to bum? Heh heh. That's a pun, Newman."

The chairs were uncomfortably close. Gino used it as an excuse to nudge his chubby little thigh against mine. "No, it's a solecism," I said, and moved my chair.

Gino was invulnerable to slights. "How would I go about getting into your company?" he asked John. "Could you put in a good word for me?"

"Are you serious?"

"Do skunks molt?"

"No, snakes molt," I told him.

"You're right. Skunks piss," he said, and returned his attention to John. "Of course I'm serious. Do you think I want to be poor all my life? Christ, I'm thirty-nine, Weiss, and I don't even own a piece of land. A guy like me, if I can't even offer a woman a roof over her head, what have I got to offer? I got fifteen thousand bucks in a retirement savings plan and my pension. That's what I've got to show for my years on the force. That and flat feet."

Now I had to feel sorry for Gino too, and for the sharp digs I'd been giving him. "But you have an interesting job, Gino," I pointed out. I was getting a case of pre-Christmas depression. Latour was dead, Ayesha was locked into a terrible emotional prison, Gino was too ugly to find a girlfriend, and poor Van Gogh was long gone. It was hard to be happy for all my own good fortune when others were so sad. Maybe I was just missing the excitement of Christmas at home. Mom would be elbow-deep in flour now. The tree would be in its usual corner, decked with all the bulbs and lights and tinsel, with the fading angel on top. People would be making mysterious and secretive trips into the house, hiding bulky parcels in closets and warning each other not to look. Neighbors would be dropping in. I didn't want to go to the Laurentians, not even if I could wear the fur coat. I wanted to go home.

When I listened into the conversation again, John was suggesting giving Bergma a call about the slides.

"For what?" Gino asked.

"It might force his hand, rattle him a little so he'd get in touch with whoever he plans to get in touch with," John explained.

"Leave it to the pros, Weiss. Patience is what we need. We'll follow all our suspects to the Laurentians. That's where they're planning to meet. Oh the Searles—their chalet is near the Pinetree Lodge. I'll pull rank and get us in there. One of the few perks of wearing a badge. Some yuppie hotshot will find himself out on his keister in the snow." He laughed with ill-natured glee.

"I wonder where the sheikh is staying," I said. "He doesn't happen to know the Searles, does he?"

"I dunno," Gino answered. "He isn't booked into any of the commercial lodges. He must know somebody. We'll just have to stick on his tail."

I didn't want John turning all protective and macho on me, but I intended to become friendly with Ayesha and find answers to some of these questions. Our pasta arrived, and we temporarily dropped the case.

CHAPTER 12

That evening, John and Gino arranged their next morning's work before Gino left. They would be doing such dull and routine things as investigating Rashid's business deals and business associates. I didn't tell them, but I intended to attack the affair from a different angle. Ayesha lived with the sheikh after all. He wouldn't tell her any criminal details, but if I could get chummy with her and win her confidence, she might let something slip. A name, a place where he could have hidden the forgeries. It seemed worth a try at least.

John mistook my silence for Christmas blues, and said, "Why don't you see if your uncle can come down and spend Christmas with us? That'd be some family for you at least."

"He's probably all booked up."

"Tell him it's on me; that might change his mind. Victor likes luxury too. It runs in the family."

"Terrific! And then I can ask him about a job for Ayesha. Oh thanks, John. I'll call him right now."

Victor is one of those kinetic people who goes to bed late and rises early, even if he doesn't have to work. By the time John left at nine, Victor would be up.

"Merry Christmas!" I chirped into the phone.

His answering voice dripped with aspartame. "Andrea, is that you? How sweet of you to call me. I meant to ring you later this morning. Did you receive the roses?"

"Victor, you old lech! It's me, Cassie!"

"Cassie! Are you in town?" The phony sweetness disappeared, replaced by genuine pleasure.

I was touched that he sounded so thrilled. "No, I'm in Montreal. What are you doing for Christmas?"

"Trying, but not too hard, to evade the clutches of a beautiful divorcée."

"Roses don't sound like evasion to me."

"For past pleasures," he said.

"What happened to Contessa Carpani?"

"The affair continues by long distance. It's costing me a fortune, but no price is too high to pay for the continued loan of the Strad."

"There ought to be a word for men like you."

"There is. Genius. Dear Maria's a charming lady, but somewhat encumbered with virtue, as Byron would say. We continue on excellent terms, however. Are you not going home for Christmas?"

"I don't think I'll make it."

"Then you must join me," he answered at once.

Christmas, the season of goodwill toward all men, was getting to him. He was lonesome for family, which was excellent. "I can't, Victor, but couldn't you join me in Montreal?"

He shivered audibly. "I hear you have subzero temperatures and yards of snow, at the moment."

"You'd never know it, here at the Ritz."

"What are you doing at the Ritz?"

I enticed him with tales of adventure and excitement and high living. It was Ayesha who finally caught his interest and won him over.

"John's company would foot the bill, you say?"

"It was his suggestion. We'd both love to see you."

"I admit I'm tempted. It could be only a short visit. I wouldn't tackle the drive, and you know I hate trains. I'll call the airport. If I can get a seat, I'll be there. I'll call you back."

Victor is very close to the top of his profession, a violin virtuoso nearly as good as he thinks he is. He could be truly great, but he caters somewhat to the squalid taste of the masses. Mom says he'll end up the Liberace of the violin. With his connections, he soon arranged a seat on a plane, even at this busy season. I arranged a room at the hotel, not on our floor.

When I remembered the one next to the sheikh was empty, I took it. John and I would meet him at Dorval that afternoon.

My next move was to figure out a way to get to Ayesha. It was too close to the hour for Madame Feydeau's tarot session to call her now. I took my tarot book down to the coffee shop to watch for Madame's arrival and, more importantly, her departure. Export A said her standing appointment was for ten. When Madame still hadn't arrived at ten-fifteen, I figured she had canceled and went upstairs to Ayesha's room.

When I tapped on the door, she came to open it herself, decked out in a white satin peignoir edged in marabou, and looking as if she had just escaped from a Jean Harlow movie. She examined me with a pair of cold, black eyes and a slight frown. She really didn't remember me.

"Good morning." I smiled, and introduced myself, reminding her where we'd met. "I lost Madame Feydeau's card, and I'm *desperate* for a reading. I was wondering if you have her number." We talked at the door; she didn't invite me in.

"She's ill today," Ayesha said, rather curtly. She was either extremely unfriendly or frightened. I soon decided it was the latter.

The door was already beginning to close. I played my trump card. "What a nuisance! And my poor uncle is flying in from Toronto. In this weather, I wanted to have a reading to make sure his flight would be safe. My uncle, Victor Mazzini," I added nonchalantly. The name obviously didn't register. "The famous violinist," I added.

The expression that claimed her features can only be described as hungry. "The Great Mazzini?" she exclaimed. "The man who was kidnapped last summer? I read of the case in Zurich. Something about a Stradivarius violin." Her voice, tinged with that classy English accent, always surprised me.

"Yes, that's the man. Such a sweetheart. I'd die if anything happened to him."

The door opened. "Come in," she smiled, wearing a whole new expression. She was eagerly excited now. I'd found the magic key to give her strength to defy Rashid. "How did you know my room?"

"Oh, everyone knows you and the sheikh," I laughed gaily. A breakfast tray was still standing on her bedside table. "I'd like a reading too," she said. "Shall we try the yellow pages and see who we can find?" While her blood-red fingernail, an inch long, coursed down the page, I took a surreptitious look around the room. She had two or three outfits tossed on the bed, apparently making her selection for the day.

"Do you read the cards at all?" I asked.

Her black mane of hair tossed a negative.

"Too bad. I was just thinking, I could read yours, and you could read mine."

"You read?" she asked, interested.

"Just an amateur."

"Why don't you give me a reading, just for fun?" she asked.

"I'd be happy to."

"Good, I'll join you in half an hour. What's your room number?"

I gave her the number and left, smiling to myself. It didn't escape my notice that the woman was self-centered, but a life of having to look out for herself could account for that. I had gone to her because I wanted a reading; she didn't care about my not getting one. She was getting what she wanted, an introduction to Victor Mazzini. Naturally I couldn't expect to peel away the result of all those years of ill treatment in five minutes. Her shyness might be part of it too. Shy people sometimes sounded curt.

I dashed back to my room and spent the interval studying the tarot book and scheming. I couldn't just blurt out a batch of questions about the sheikh the minute she sat down. He'd have to show up in the cards. The Lovers, from the Major Arcana, seemed a likely possibility. The Hanged Man would be useful too. He could be interpreted as foretelling large changes in one's life, a bettering of one's condition, a getting rid of difficulties. In short, ditching the sheikh and becoming an actress.

I thought Ayesha was the kind of woman who would spend hours at her toilette, and fully expected she'd be late. She caught me offguard by arriving fifteen minutes early, and of course looking gorgeous. She was all in subtle taupe suede with a tailored silk shirt the dusty brown shade of powdered cocoa.

She smiled broadly, but it was only a lip smile. Her luminous black eyes were busy scanning the room. "Is your John out?" she asked.

"Yes, on business, but his name's Sean." Oh my God, did she know who he really was?

She blinked, and in that blinking of an eye I realized my error. She was speaking hookerese. I laughed uneasily. "My John's not here. I guess we can call a spade a spade, since we're alone."

"For small mercies," she said, and lounged at her ease on the bed, where she kicked off a pair of alligator pumps. "Where did you meet yours?"

That "small mercies" I found revealing. She really disliked her work. Naturally she talked like a hooker; she was one, but that didn't mean she was all bad. I decided to stick to the truth as much as possible, to avoid verbal difficulties. "Toronto, last summer."

"What are you going to do with him when Mazzini arrives?"

"Oh, my uncle knows about Sean."

"Really?" She blinked again, and looked confused. "Is he *really* an uncle then, or do the three of you . . ."

"He's my uncle."

She looked more confused than ever. "I just wondered. Some men like—well, you know. Awful what some women have to put up with." She gave a little shiver, and suddenly looked about twelve years old. What had this child had to put up with that had turned her into a zombie?

She smiled wanly. "A man like Mazzini must lead an interesting life, travel a lot. Is he—nice?"

"He's charming. He travels mostly on his concert tours." I could almost hear her gears grinding. She'd like to ditch Rashid and join up with Victor. Nobody could be as rich as Rashid. What did he do to her that she'd be so eager to switch? "He mingles with all the performing crowd—actors, directors, TV producers. Are you not happy with the sheikh?" I ventured, chummily, as one hooker to another.

She tossed her shoulders. "I've been with him over a year. He's generous—very generous, but the man's a demon of jealousy! He wouldn't even like my seeing you. What's yours like?"

"Not as wealthy as the sheikh, of course, but generous within his means."

"I notice he gave you a nice fur," she said calmly. I felt soiled, talking to her. "What does he do?"

"He's a businessman," I said vaguely. "Oil—Texas."

She examined her long nails. "It's nice in the States, but I hope you don't have to live in Texas. New York, L.A., I wouldn't mind that. I'm trying to get Rashid to buy a condo in L.A."

My emotions went on a roller-coaster ride as they switched from pity to disdain. What had I expected? That a woman who'd been living in the lap of luxury for a few years would be like an ordinary teenager? "Are you interested in movie work?" I asked casually.

Her strangely impassive face showed a spark of life. "Legitimate movies, yes. Not blue films."

Knowing her past, I was careful not to denigrate blue films. "A girl has to start somewhere," I said.

"I played Juliet once, just in a school play. I wasn't very good, but I enjoyed it. Acting is difficult. Enough bull. Let's get on with the reading," she said. "Have you got anything to smoke?"

"I don't smoke."

"I've got some pot in my room. If you like . . ." She jumped up, eager to please.

"No, I'm fine."

"Let's have something to drink," was her next desire.

"There's some Scotch . . ."

"I don't like the hard stuff."

I didn't like to suggest champagne and whipped cream at ten-thirty in the morning. "Coffee?" I said doubtfully.

"Great." She lifted the phone and ordered a pot.

It was time to begin the reading. "I'll let you establish the aura while we wait," she suggested. "I'll get the coffee."

I took my queue and and went into John's sitting room, where the reading would occur. I closed the curtains to eliminate distractions, as dictated in my book. Knowing she could see me from the bedroom, I stood still and did some deep breathing, ostensibly to self-energize my mind. I was not so deep into meditation that I failed to hear the coffee arrive, and the delighted thanks when Ayesha handed the guy a tip. My book didn't say anything about having coffee while reading the cards, but apparently Madame Feydeau allowed herself this dispensation, and I did likewise.

I shuffled and cut the deck five times while Ayesha poured. When I was done, I put the deck on the table, face down. Ayesha, the seeker of knowledge, was supposed to allow me fifteen minutes before she started peppering me with questions.

"Shall I spread?" I asked.

"Please. Let's just do a Major Arcana."

This was music to my ears. I lifted the large, cumbersome deck and sorted out the proper cards. They were very colorful and ornate, with the major figures surrounded by occult symbols. I cut them into three piles to Ayesha's left, with my left hand. This is a strict rule, and holds the key to success. Next I stacked the three piles so that the card on Ayesha's right was on top, also de rigueur. I decided to flip sideways, rather than up and over. Dealer's choice. I chatted as I lay out the spread, to establish rapport with the seeker and the occult forces. My attempts to explain the meaning of the septenaries, the twenty-two cards of the Major Arcana plus The Fool, which I hoped I wouldn't call the Joker, was cut short by an impatient, "Yes, yes. I know all that. Let's get on with it."

I figured maybe the sheikh would be calling, and she was afraid to be gone for long from her room. "Madame Feydeau uses a circular spread. Can't you use it?" she asked.

I had laid them out in a line, but I knew real readers stuck to one method, and said, "No, I follow this system."

Long before the quarter of an hour was up, Ayesha began exclaiming excitedly and shooting questions at me. She seemed youthful and enthusiastic, completely different from when she was with Rashid. "The World comes up first. That never happened before!" she said. "What does it mean? A reward—doesn't it mean a reward?"

"It's reversed," I pointed out, surprised she hadn't noticed it, as this card is a nude woman, surrounded by symbols. "It means confusion, destruction—if you're afraid of change," I added slyly. I meant to impress the need for a change of lifestyle.

"I love change. I'm due for a change, past due. If only I

could get away from Rashid! But he's very influential. Look, the Star is right beside the World, it's not reversed. What does that mean?''

"Hope, despite difficulties. A new beginning for you."

"What about Rashid? Dare I leave him?" she asked, with fear glowing in her eyes. Her eyes moved to the Lovers, a naked man and woman, backed by the tree of life. "It's not reversed. That would indicate a rupture, but this means two hearts in harmony. The male is stronger . . ."

"But the female has a strong mind too," I said. "And a decision must be made to find happiness."

"What about the Hangman? He's the card of happenings," she said eagerly.

"He's reversed, and right next to the Lovers," I said. "That could be . . ." Disaster! No, I didn't want to talk her out of leaving Rashid. I lit on the High Priestess, right beside the Hangman. "Strong self-reliance here," I said firmly, and went on to substantiate this by the Empress and her love of creativity, also upright.

Ayesha returned to the Hangman. "Death—does it mean I'm going to die?" Her soft voice was hushed. She actually believed this stuff.

"No, Death is the skeleton knight on horseback. And he's not reversed. It means rebirth, a new beginning. Perhaps a new career . . ."

"Madame said the reversed Hangman could mean death."

"Everyone interprets the cards slightly differently. Why should you be afraid of death? You're young and healthy."

"I'm going to die young," she said, in a flat, resigned voice, as if she were saying it's December or I'm Irish. Just stating a fact.

"Did Madame say so?"

"No, my aunt told me. I used to visit her in London."

I quickly mussed up the cards. "I wouldn't take all this too seriously, Ayesha. It's just a game."

She stared as though I were a lunatic. "Fortune-telling was good enough for Plato and Aristotle. It's good enough for me."

"Plato?"

"Oh certainly. Pythagoras too."

"That was a long time ago. They still thought the world was flat and gods lived on Olympus."

Ayesha lifted the pot and poured more coffee. Her hand was trembling. She stood up suddenly with her full cup and accidentally sloshed half of it on me. Fortunately it was no longer hot enough to burn, but she'd wrecked my new pinstripe slacks that I couldn't even wash.

"Oh I'm sorry! So clumsy of me," she said, and began pulling tissues out of her Gucci purse to blot at me.

"It's all right; I'll change."

I made a quick trip to my bedroom and changed slacks. She was still at the table when I returned. Her nerves seemed to have settled down. "When is your uncle coming?" she asked.

"This afternoon. Would you like to meet him?"

She was all eyes. "Could I?"

"I'm sure he'd love to meet you. He has an eye for the ladies."

"And he knows the movie crowd, you said?"

"Yes, and they're making a lot of movies in Toronto nowadays."

She nodded, interested. "Rashid adores the violin, so he won't refuse an invitation. He makes me go to concerts." But apparently she wouldn't be let out alone where she might meet people other than store clerks. I thought having a go at Rashid might help John and invented a party on the spot. "We're having a little cocktail party to welcome him this evening," I said. "I do hope you can come."

"Where, here at the hotel?"

"Yes—I'll let you know the exact time and place."

"We're going to dinner at eight-thirty. Some business associates of Rashid's. He'll make me go to that."

"Yes, we're going out too. It'll be earlier. Around six," I said vaguely.

"Super. So where are you going from here?" was her next question, one much to my liking.

"I hope somewhere for a little skiing; then back to Texas. How about you and Rashid?" I could ask, with no cause for suspicion.

"London."

Not skiing? Had Rashid ordered her to lie if anyone asked? "Do you spend a lot of time in Europe?"

"As much as possible, preferably in Paris, and of course Milan for the shows. Rashid doesn't mind that. He likes Armani himself."

Ah, then it was fashion shows we were talking about. "Sean prefers Cardin," I replied, and turned to other Italian goodies. "Do you and Rashid like art, at all? I just wondered, since you mentioned Italy."

"Rashid has a villa full of paintings on the Riviera. A lot of Picassos and the Impressionists."

"Oh, I love the Impressionists. Who does he collect—Renior, Monet . . . ?"

She nodded. "The Post-Impressionists too. He adores Van Gogh."

I was careful not to choke on my coffee. "They're worth millions now," I said, fully impressed.

"He can still afford them. He's very rich. But with all that money, he never gives me a penny. Just credit cards," she sighed.

"I never heard the sheikh was a collector."

"He keeps it quiet. Afraid of robbery, I suppose." She hunched an elegant suede shoulder. "Or perhaps for other reasons. It might be best not to inquire where he got some of the pictures."

I stored all this up for John and began fishing to discover something about her origins. "Where did you meet him, Ayesha?"

"In London, I went to school there. My father was attached to the diplomatic corps. I met up with him again later in Paris."

"Oh, I see." There went my theory of a deprived childhood. "What nationality are you?"

"Part Ay-rab," she said, smiling, "and part Korean, on my mom's side. She's dead."

"I'm sorry. Has she been dead long?"

"She committed suicide eight years ago. She was mentally unstable and hated England. I think the fog killed her." Her crust of indifference was cracking, to show the troubled girl beneath the veneer. Her fingers moved nervously over the tarot cards.

"What does your dad think of how you live now?"

She shrugged. "I wouldn't know. I haven't been in touch with him since I ran away from finishing school in Switzerland when I was sixteen, just after Mom's death. I went with a rock star," she said, shaking her head sadly. "All the girls talked about doing it. I was the only one foolish enough to do it. It seemed a good idea at the time. I only did it to impress the other girls. They were so snooty to a foreigner. Sex and drugs and rock 'n' roll. You'll do anything when you need a fix. But I'm clean now, except for a little toke once in a while. Shall I get some?"

Sixteen and eight, she was twenty-four, no longer a delinquent child. But I still had to pity her. She had probably been very attached to her mother and had become a little unstable herself when her mother committed suicide. Her life might be a kind of revenge on her father for having kept his wife in London, which she apparently hated. Ayesha wasn't the first girl to fall victim to sex and drugs and rock 'n' roll, not necessarily in that order.

"Not for me, thanks. I guess you really miss your mother at a time like this. Christmas, I mean."

Ayesha was becoming fidgety. I wondered if it was only an occasional toke she indulged in. She really looked zonked at times. That would account for the air of boredom. She stood up and shrugged. "Christmas was no big deal with us. We're not Christians. Rashid is giving me a Rolls. Bribery—he knows I want to leave him. I did, a while ago. He had me brought back."

It was hard to know what to reply to this generous tyranny. "Wow! A Rolls! What will you do with it, when you travel so much?"

"I'd like to leave him and drive to L.A. Look, about Mazzini, if I'm out, you can leave a message at the desk. I'd really like to meet him. I better go now. Thanks for the reading, Cathy."

She left, and I stood looking at the paneled door. She didn't even remember my name. Had drugs ruined her mind? I'd have to warn Victor the lady was troubled. Maybe she needed psychiatric help, after what she'd been through. I'd try to help her get into a career, but I wouldn't let Victor run any risks in the doing.

More importantly, I had added a piece to the case. Sheikh Rashid was a collector of paintings, not necessarily come by honestly. If we failed to find the paintings here, the originals would eventually end up in the sheikh's Riviera mansion, from which it wouldn't be impossible to rescue them. I was still congratulating myself when John returned around noon.

He glanced at the table and the two coffee cups and tarot cards. "Company?" he asked, quirking an eyebrow at me.

"Yes, I gave a reading to a friend."

"I'm glad to know I'm engaged to an enlightened, educated lady. Don't tell me you believe that stuff?"

"If it was good enough for Plato . . ."

He snorted and glanced at his little overnight bag, which was at the end of the sofa. "I wish you'd keep that thing closed," he said. "I've got the slides I stole from Bergma in there."

"I didn't touch them. You must have left it open yourself."

His look expressed his opinion of this impossible lapse of care. "I hid them under my BVD's and closed the case. I didn't think I had to lock it."

"But I didn't touch it, John!"

"Then the maid's been rifling it. I often wondered if they snoop."

He lifted the case. The slides were sticking up through the underwear, and the case wasn't properly closed. We exchanged a look.

"Whose fortune were you telling?"

I gulped. "Ayesha's. And it really worked, John. Rashid has an art collection in a mansion on the Riviera. He collects hot stuff. He practically keeps her prisoner."

He looked unimpressed. "If you tell me she spilt coffee on you and you had to change . . ."

He knew the answer without my having to say anything. "Victor's coming," I offered, as an apology.

"Much good it'll do us now! She'll have notified Rashid we're on to him."

"I'm sure she won't. She doesn't even like him. She wants to leave him," I said, and revealed all my dark secrets.

"That's great, Honey, but next time . . ." He looked for-lornly at the slides.

"I didn't know you put them under your undies. What a dumb place to hide them."

"You're right. I should have warned you and hid the case."

"I don't think she was interested in the slides at all. She was probably just trying to find out how rich you are. She asked about you."

"Maybe. Did this talk of Rashid's collection come up before or after she searched my case."

"After. Now she wouldn't have gone telling me all that if she suspected anything. I bet she didn't even glance at them. She could have taken them if she was suspicious. Maybe she just pulled open the box to see if there was any coke in it. I think she might be an addict. She used to be anyway. It's a tough habit to break."

John thought about it for a moment. "Well, she wouldn't have told you about Rashid's collection if she was suspicious. What time's Victor arriving?"

"Three-thirty, at Dorval."

He glanced at his watch. "Just time for lunch. Gino says there's a nice spot called Tuesday, on Crescent."

"That's Thursday's. Very nice, and close too. We can walk, in the fur coat."

"I doubt it'll fit me."

"True, and you'd probably prefer a sheepskin anyway. You know—wolf, sheep's clothing. Never mind, it wasn't very funny."

He smiled dutifully and helped me into the fur.

CHAPTER 13

After lunch, Menard whisked us out to Dorval Airport, where we had to wait nearly an hour for Victor's plane. All the planes were running late and were crowded to the gills at the busy holiday season. Victor was easy to recognize amidst the throng of hurrying passengers. He looked like some minor European royalty, with his finely chiseled face, topped by a beaver hat. His mink-lined overcoat, rather long, flapped open as he walked. He removed the hat and smoothed his silver hair, while his black, alley-cat eyes scanned the crowd to see if anyone had recognized him. I don't think anyone did, but he's the kind of man you look at twice. Even if you don't know quite who he is, you sense he's somebody.

There's an air of drama about him. He's still handsome too, for a man his age. His age! He'd hate that description! On him, fifty looks young. He's lean and swarthy enough that his noble features appear tanned in all seasons.

"Victor! Victor! Over here!" I shouted.

He spotted me and came barging forward for a bear hug. He smelled delicious. Victor wears zircon "diamonds," but for his scent, he insists on the genuine thing. After a flurry of "Merry Christmas" and "How are you?" and "How was your trip?" we decided to wait in the bar till the departing crowd thinned. Not that it would really, but it made a good excuse to go to the bar. That interest in the stomach must run in the family. The pit stop was Victor's suggestion.

"It'll give John a chance to tell me what the hell's going on," Victor said, leading us all merrily off in the wrong direction. There was a blonde in Godiva-like tresses down to her swinging rump a few paces ahead of him. Another of Victor's little weaknesses.

I squeezed his arm and headed him toward the bar. "Easy on the sauce, Uncle," I whispered. Victor has been known to imbibe more than is good for him.

"Sauce bedamned. It's a cigar I want. They don't let you smoke on the plane."

We ordered coffee, and Victor assuaged his urged for a Havana. "I shouldn't have coffee, with my high blood pressure," he said, "but since I've been ordered to cut down, I crave it more than ever. Why couldn't broccoli be bad for you?"

I ordered decaf and switched my cup with his, assuming it was the caffeine that was restricted.

His black eyes sparkled like diamonds. "A sheikh, an oriental porn queen, a murder, forged Van Goghs, a dire plot to swindle a museum—it doesn't sound too boring," he nodded.

"And now a world-class violinist to lend us a touch of class," I added.

"Best of all, I stay free at the Ritz. Ha ha." This brought not only a smile but a burst of delighted laughter. Right in the middle of it, his lips closed and a frown drew his brows together. "Where'd you get that coat?" he demanded. For about twenty seconds, I noticed a resemblance to my mother, who is about as unlike her brother Victor as it is possible for two siblings to be.

John flew to my defense. "It's rented. I'm posing as a Texas oilman. Cassie's my . . ."

"Secretary!" I threw in hastily. Oh dear, the adjoining rooms! I must remember to lock the door while Victor was around.

"Rented? Deductible, I suppose?" he asked John.

"Right, and the diamonds you'll be seeing tonight are paste."

"Diamonds are a man's worst enemy. Nobody but an idiot wastes money on real diamonds. They don't pay interest, and they don't keep pace with inflation."

"We rented a Caddie limo too," I said. That suited Victor right down to the ground.

"Since I'll be arriving in style," he decided, "why not call the press and create a little stir in the lobby? It might impress your Dragon Lady."

He bobbed off and made a few calls. Publicity is a part of any performing artist's career, I suppose. With Victor, it was a mania. He was always good copy. A skirt-chasing, cigar-smoking, wine-drinking famous violinist with a temperament slightly wilder than Maria Callas's makes a lively story.

Not only the newspapers but the TV cameras were outside the Ritz to greet him as we stepped forth from the limo. As if the whole thing had been arranged by a producer, Ayesha was just returning from one of her shopping binges. She stopped and stared at all the cameras. I noticed her adjust her silken ebony hair artfully over her shoulders and arrange a smile before she went into camera range. She soon singled out the cause of the small furor and examined Victor.

When she spotted me, she came swanning forward. "The Great Mazzini?" she asked.

"Yes. I can't imagine how the press found out he was coming. He must have told someone in Toronto before he left. He'll be annoyed."

Her obsidian eyes strayed to John. I read the message glinting in them, beneath her lowered lashes. Her smile, when I introduced them, was shy but provocative. John, being very human, was not unmoved by the look. His mustache curved in pleasure.

"So you're Sean Bradley," she said, in that high-class accent. "I've heard so much about you, Sean."

He gave his boyish smile, teeth slightly overlapping in front to add a guileless air, and said, "Not the truth, I hope."

A low croon gurgled in her throat. "You lucky woman, Cathy," she said, sparing a glance at me. Her blood red fingernails had strayed to John's arm, where they rested lightly.

"The name's Cassie, actually," I reminded her.

Before sterner measures, like maybe a half nelson, were called for, she turned her attention to Victor. "Is Mazzini giving a concert?" she asked over her shoulder. "How I'd love to hear him play."

"No, it's just a family visit," I told her.

"I caught him at Avery Fisher Hall last year—Mozart. The Violin Concerto, no. 3 in G, I believe it was—it caused goose bumps all over." She squirmed her shoulders and batted her eyes at John. Even I could picture her lovely naked body, covered in nothing but gooseflesh. What had made me think she was shy? And how had she suddenly become an encyclopedia of music? She had implied earlier that Rashid forced her to go to concerts. She must have been picking his brains to impress Victor.

We all squeezed into the lobby and the reporters began firing questions at Victor, while bulbs popped and cameras whirred. Victor was in his element: a world-class hotel, an exotic beauty drooling all over him, and mega-press to record it all for posterity. He was in no hurry to leave, and neither was Ayesha. No introduction was made, but she said before leaving, "What time is your little party, Cassie?"

"Six-thirty. We've hired a parlor here in the hotel. Will the sheikh be coming?"

"We're both looking forward to it."

She blew a kiss at the party in general and strode away, her wolf coat swaying behind her like an emperor's robe.

John got Victor's key from the desk, and we went upstairs to wait for him. I spent the time arranging details for the party. It was nothing elaborate, just the few friends and colleagues Victor could scrape up in a hurry. When Victor came upstairs, he began making the necessary calls to the guests, and John and I went to our rooms to hide any evidence of mutual visits. Export A soon came and peeked his head in.

"What's shaking, folks?" he asked.

"You tell us," John said. "Is the sheikh in?"

"Not 'less he came down the chimney. He hasn't been through the lobby. I hear you folks are having a party."

"I wonder where Ayesha went this afternoon," I said, looking a question at him.

"I don't know where else she was, but since you're interested, I took a look at the bag she was carrying. It said the Museum of Fine Arts. They have a little shop there—sell books, reproductions of paintings and artworks. Stuff like that. Nothing very valuable."

I gave John a meaningful look.

"It was a real small bag," Export A added. "Maybe one of their arty calendars. Gotta go now, folks." He left.

"Or maybe she was carrying a letter," I suggested.

John's eyes narrowed and his mustache bristled with eagerness. "We'd better have her followed in future as well. Not that she'd be up to anything herself. She looks kind of—vulnerable, doesn't she?" His approval of the woman had the curious effect of making me suspect her of heinous crimes. "Rashid could be using her to carry messages though. He and Bergma certainly aren't communicating in person or by phone. If Gino can't come up with another man, I'll have Menard tail her. In a pinch, I can always drive the limo myself. I wouldn't mind getting behind that wheel."

"You harbor a death wish, do you?"

"Gino's supposed to phone at five. I'll ask him if his man at the museum saw Ayesha speaking to Bergma."

Instead of phoning, Gino decided to call in person. His nose was red and his eyes were watering. "Christ, I wish I'd get transferred to Victoria, B.C.," he said, swatting at his body with his arms. "Try to get a cab in this town. My dad needed his car. I've been busting my bunions standing on street corners waiting for a bus while the polar wind blows through me. If God had meant for me to walk, he would have given me longer legs. And if He'd meant for us to live in the arctic, he'd have given us pelts. You got a drink, Weiss? My veins are frozen solid."

"Can't you get an RCMP car?" I asked.

"They're already ticked off that I was parachuted in on them. They're being about as helpful as a cellophane hankie. All they have available, they tell me, is marked cars."

"Hire a car," John suggested.

"It isn't worth the paperwork."

He took the proffered glass of Scotch and belted it down straight. When his veins had defrosted, he said, "The sheikh's lady turned up at the museum this afternoon."

"So I hear," John said. "Did she speak to anyone interesting?"

"Not Bergma. He was taking some bunch of blue-haired ladies through the Art Nouveau show. She hung around a while, not paying any special attention to him. I don't think they exchanged a single glance. Then she went up to the coffee shop, had a coffee—alone—went to the little art store, and bought a pen.''

''Did she use it?'' John asked swiftly.

''If she did, she used it in the can. That was her only stop before she left. Bergma's secretary was in there at the same time.''

''Hot Buns!'' I exclaimed, adrenaline pumping. ''Who went in first, Ayesha or Hot Buns?''

Gino wrinkled his brow. ''Hot Buns. Ayesha could have followed her and passed along a message from Rashid.''

John dealt a blow of frustration to his own knee and said, ''Damn! Now we'll never know what was in it.''

I felt a eureka feeling coming over me. ''We're fools! They could have been corresponding by letter all along. Is their mail searched, Gino?''

''No, we figured at Christmas, the mail's so slow they wouldn't resort to letters.''

''There's always messenger service,'' John pointed out. His face was red, which meant he was cursing himself for this oversight. ''Cassie, would you mind calling Export A and see if Rashid has used any messenger service since he's been here, and if so, which one?''

I made the call immediately. Export A said he'd look into it and get back to me, which he did, with astonishing promptitude. ''Loomis, nine times!'' is all he said.

Gino bounced up from his chair as if he was on a spring and darted downstairs, presumably to dash off to Loomis Messenger Service and flash his badge to get addresses.

I arranged myself comfortably on John's bed and said, ''Bergma or Hot Buns might have been using a messenger service too, John.''

''We can't very well demand their records without blowing the whole thing. There must be dozens of messenger services in Montreal. It'll take days to check it out. They've put one over on us. While we've sat on their tails and monitored phones, they've been corresponding by messenger. They could even have sent the paintings on ahead somewhere by messenger or mail. They sure as hell haven't turned up in any of the places they should have.''

"They could even have sent them on to the sheikh's villa on the Riviera."

John grabbed the phone and placed a call to a real estate agent in Cannes. He spoke in reasonably good French for about five minutes, sometimes just waiting impatiently for a minute or so, and then hung up. "Just checking to see that Rashid *does* have a villa on the Riviera," he explained. "I know a real estate agent there, Henri Villiers. He says Rashid does own a little place, a three-bedroom cottage he visits about a week a year. It doesn't seem a likely spot to hold a famous collection of paintings. He doesn't have a housekeeper. The place is empty fifty-one weeks a year. No renovations were done when he bought it from a schoolteacher. Rashid's been feeding Ayesha a line, Cassie. Now isn't that interesting."

"Or maybe she was feeding me one. And she did it after spilling coffee all over my new slacks and looking at the slides, the bitch. She knows all about Rashid's business."

"That's possible," John admitted reluctantly, pulling at his mustache to hide his shame at being temporarily blinded by her beauty. "Either the Mounties or I will definitely have to spring for another tail. She's been running loose all the time. Rashid must have had her dump the paintings somewhere."

"I followed her part of the time. She certainly didn't mail anything then. I wonder what they'd use. Either the post office or a messenger. Ayesha didn't mention going skiing before they left Canada, but they have skis. She said they're going to London. I wonder if the pictures have been shipped to whatever ski chalet they plan to visit."

"That'd be why she claimed London as the next stop. Maybe Victor could get something out of them."

"Did I tell you Rashid bought her a Rolls for Christmas?"

"Three times."

"I'm not hinting. I just wondered if she'd actually got it yet. I haven't seen her drive it."

"Maybe it's just ordered, or maybe it's being prepped."

"That wouldn't prevent her from stashing a few pictures in the trunk, would it?"

He lifted the phonebook. "There wouldn't be more than one Rolls dealer in town."

"This looks like another job for super-Gino."

"I'll lend him the limo. Poor blighter; he'll freeze his tail trying to hail a cab in weather like this."

When Gino returned, he said, "Rashid made plenty of use of messengers all right, all for business stuff. Lawyers and real estate people. Nothing to Bergma or the museum."

"Maybe he used his own private messenger—Ayesha," John said. "She'd do it if he told her to. She's scared stiff of him." He discussed with Gino what we'd been talking about.

Gino shook his head. "I'm dipping pretty heavy into the Mounties' personnel pool already. They won't go for lending me another man."

"Ever driven a Caddie limo?" John asked.

Gino looked at the ceiling and smiled. "Only in my dreams."

"You can tell Menard he has a new job, tailing Ayesha, and you take the Caddie down to the Rolls dealer. See if Rashid bought the woman a Rolls, and if he did, check it out, especially the trunk."

"Caddies, Rolls, jeez, this sounds like fairyland. You got it made in the shade, Weiss. Wouldn't I love to get my hands on a Rolls-Royce and the women that drive them. That Ayesha, what a dish. Did you ever notice the way she tosses her head, with all that black hair flying around? And the fingernails—an inch long I swear. Never a chip out of them. Makeup all in place, shiny as a new Rolls herself."

"But the upholstery's more like a Caddie," John grinned.

"You said it. In another ten years, she'll be all ass. I like well-upholstered women."

He tossed a disparaging eye over my meager frame, reached for the Scotch bottle, and poured himself a shot. "I guess you don't want me hanging around for the violinist's party, eh? Not classy enough for you guys."

"Why not?" John asked. I knew he was feeling sorry for Gino. "But keep a low profile, huh?"

Gino looked from his toes up along the short length of his body and said, "Do I have any choice? Don't be afraid that I'll disgrace you. I'll make sure I spit into the spittoon. I wouldn't want to get the ladies' legs wet." Every day, in every way, he became grosser and grosser. "I'm getting myself a new blazer for Christmas. Crest, brass buttons, the works."

Awful visions of Gino in a fifty-five dollar blazer, gleaming with brass, flashed through my head. For some reason, I saw him in a captain's hat, which was ridiculous. He probably would wear brown shoes though, and polyester trousers.

"If my profile becomes too high and anybody actually notices me, you can say I'm a poor relation," he said, and left.

"Speaking of relations," I said, "I'd better give Victor a call. And remember, John, this door is kept severely locked till he leaves."

"Just so I get to keep the key," he grinned.

About ten minutes later, I escaped reluctantly from his arms and went to get ready for the cocktail party and to call Victor.

CHAPTER 14

I am not really so empty-headed that I crave nothing but glamour in my life. Family is important, love, learning, doing good deeds upon occasion. I have a social conscience. I have been known to write letters to newspapers and congressmen and congresswomen. I sign those petitions with whose aims I agree, and have even stood on street corners, pen and paper in hand, soliciting signatures. Which is not to say I don't love glamour. I do. For me, it is the icing on the cake, and tonight's cake promised to hold lavish icing indeed.

I would be in my element and would dress for the part. I opted for the white cocktail dress, a nifty little crepe spaghetti-strap number that hugged the body tight all over, only relenting with a burst of ruffle at the bottom, to allow a stride longer than six inches. It would have looked better with a tan, but tans are no longer compulsory, since the surge in skin cancer. With three or four ounces of good imitation jewelry clinging to my neck and wrists, I was ready to take on the international world of crime.

Victor always looks super, especially when he's out for a night on the town. I didn't mind a bit that he'd gone whole hog and wore a black formal suit with ruffled shirtfront. We could always say he was dining out later. And John—gorgeous in his formal suit too. He'd come a long way from Plains, Nebraska. Even Gino looked decent. Heff would have been proud of him. The blazer wasn't made-to-measure, but it must

132

have undergone extensive alterations. The cuffs weren't too long, the hem didn't ride below his tailbone, and the crest wasn't that gaudy. Best of all, he'd bought new gray flannels and black shoes. I didn't know they made men's oxfords in such a small size. You could see his yellow sox only when he sat down.

He tossed his coat on the bed and did a pirouette for us. "Does it meet with your approval, Ms. Newman?" he asked. His proud little face assumed a positive, indeed an enthusiastic response.

I gave him thumbs up. "Aces, Parelli. Santa Claus did you proud."

"Santa my ass. This rig set me back a hundred and fifty bucks. Can you imagine, a hundred and fifty bucks for a jacket? If Ma knew, she'd have me committed."

"Then we won't tell her. Gentlemen, shall we go down?"

To enter a lobby surrounded by a phalanx of gentlemen, two-thirds of whom look downright distinguished, is an experience never to be forgotten. For about two minutes, I felt the way Liz Taylor must feel all the time. Envied, gaped at, and knowing I looked great. The hormones and adrenaline and other beneficial chemicals rushing through my veins gave me a natural high.

Black-coated waiters bowed and said, "This way, Ms. Newman," and cast darting smiles at Victor. Export A stood in the background, greeting me with a big wink and an OK sign. In the center of the small parlor a bar had been set up. There wasn't much else in the room except some chairs along the walls, but it was a classy room with big gilt-framed paintings and a Persian carpet.

Victor was in his element, behaving like a Parisian boulevardier, kissing ladies' hands and smiling with silken insincerity at their husbands. I got to be the hostess, greeting guests and shaking hands and saying in my most polite accents, "So glad you could come on such short notice." As I didn't actually know the celebrities whose hands I was pumping so warmly, Victor made me acquainted. Symphony conductors, other musicians, several reporters, a glamorous lady or two who turned out to be from CBC, and their escorts, one of whom I recognized from TV.

I felt I had strolled right into an evening soap opera. When at last the sheikh and Ayesha arrived, a breathless hush fell over the party. The sheikh hadn't dressed for the occasion, but Ayesha had decided to set off her oriental charms in some glowing drapery akin to a sari, and looked fantastic. She was in white too, which showed me how much better the tan actually set it off than my wanly tinted skin. She was dripping in emeralds and had her hair pulled back. I hadn't realized before that her neck was so long and swanlike. The flowing robes hid her one flaw, the wide stern.

She introduced Sheikh Rashid to us. He gave a slightly bored look that was perhaps meant as a smile and bowed his head in a regal way. I felt he was present under duress and would make a hasty exit. There I was mistaken. He liked Victor's work; Victor liked his money and woman. With these natural attractions going for them, they got along like a house on fire. He got Victor aside and for half an hour I heard crumbs of conversation featuring such technical details as "Nothing like a Stradivarius for tone," "left-hand technique," "bow speed and pressure," and "the magical enamel has never been matched," "speed patterns," "Oh yes, the Carpani Strad, from Italy."

They discussed the late Jascha Heifetz. "A flawless intonation, dazzling performance, incredible dexterity," the sheikh said.

"But a cold man," Victor countered. Praise for another's work was anathema to him, unless he introduced the praise himself, in which case lukewarm agreement was all that was required.

"I never met him," the sheikh said sadly.

"The Garbo of the violin," Victor sympathized. "He valued his privacy. I always felt he considered playing a duty. Now I'll tell you who is coming on and he actually enjoys himself at it is young Cho-Liang-Lin—we call him Jimmy. An Oriental—Taiwan, I believe."

"Yes, we were fortunate enough to catch him in Paris. I put him in the first rank for his age. He'll be another Perlman or Zukerman. I read in the *Strad* that he studied with Dorothy DeLay."

"Ah, you read our *Bible!*" Victor beamed. He had a real expert by the toe here.

Seeing that the conversation might go on forever, I sidled over to Ayesha, who had got the ear (and eyes and arm and probably heart) of the TV actor.

"There's loads of work for actresses now," he was assuring her. "They make all those romance videos here in Montreal, you know, some of them with very well known movie actors. My agent wants me to star in one. You'd be perfect for the female lead. She isn't cast yet."

"But I'm not a WASP!" she laughed.

His face melted at the sound. "No, you're a lotus flower." She gave him a stunned look.

Gino sidled up to me and said, "How am I doing, Newman?"

"I don't see any wet marks on the ladies."

Ayesha left the actor and joined us. This surprised me. I thought she had found a useful partner. Apparently she considered romance videos beneath her. "Dreadful man," she said. "He makes videos."

I presented Gino, explaining that he was "Sean's" assistant, in case she wondered at seeing him around the hotel.

"I hear you're a Shakespearean actress, Ms. Hejaz," Gino smiled.

"I told him about your playing Juliet," I explained.

"In what, if I may ask?" Gino said, trying to look suave.

She looked at me, stupefied. *"Hamlet,"* I said.

"One of my own personal faves," Gino nodded.

Even this scintillating conversation wasn't enough to keep her from Victor. She soon joined him and Rashid, and gazed as though mesmerized at my uncle. I didn't like to interrupt the bond Victor was forging with Rashid, but eventually I had to draw his attention to the other guests, some of whom could only stay half an hour. Most of them were on their way to another party. The last to leave were Rashid and Ayesha.

Rashid was gushing like a schoolgirl. That fatuous smile removed any aura of mystery or danger from him. "I can never tell you how much I regret that you didn't bring your Stradivarius with you," the sheikh said. "I shall call on you in Toronto the next time I'm there and hear you play that transcription of the *Emperor Concerto* you promised me. You won't forget, my flat in Paris is always at your disposal. I'll notify my housekeeper to welcome you at any time. It has been an honor to meet you, Mr. Mazzini. A great honor. I wish I didn't have to leave, but business . . .''

A ski trip was hardly "business," unless it involved the paintings too.

"Perhaps we can get together again before you leave town," Victor said.

"Alas, this lady is dragging me up to the Laurentians for Christmas," Rashid smiled wanly at Ayesha. "And till then, I'll be rushing to finalize this little real estate deal."

I tried not to give a jerk of surprise at the sheikh admitting to the ski trip, when Ayesha had hidden it.

"I'm thinking of taking a jaunt up to the ski hills myself," Victor said. "Where are you staying?"

Rashid didn't hesitate a second before answering. "The Staynors, business friends, have invited us to their lodge. I wish I could ask you to come along, but it is not my party. We're dining with them this evening. We really must dash. We're late already."

They left, and the rest of us gathered in a clump on the chairs around the edge of the room.

"The sheikh admitted to the ski trip!" I told John.

"Yes, we know where they're going from here," Victor said. "To visit the Staynors, unless he lied. He seemed pretty upfront, don't you think? Damned decent of him to put his Paris flat at my disposal."

"Nobody ever offers me a free holiday in Paris," Gino said forlornly. "Oh by the way, Weiss, the sheikh did buy the girl a Rolls. White Corniche, a neat little convertible. Paid cash—a check I mean. It's supposed to be delivered on December the twenty-fourth, tomorrow, in time for Christmas. The trunk and everything else in it was clean. She just went down and picked it out, and hasn't been back since, not even to drool over it. Imagine, he's giving her a Rolls-Royce, and what does she do to earn it? As if we didn't know."

Victor shook his head. "I can't believe Rashid's mixed up in this business. A man who appreciates music like that. A

refined, sensitive soul, and too rich to have to steal anything.
Isn't there anyone else it could be?''

"Let's go somewhere more private to talk," John suggested.

It was so perishing cold out that we decided to have dinner
in the hotel dining room. "Is this on you, Weiss?" Gino asked,
before accepting an invitation to join us.

"It's the company's treat," John told him.

"Did you remember to put in a word for me?"

"I will, when I get back to the office, Gino," John promised.

Over the crab legs Victor said, "You didn't answer my
question, John. Don't you have any other suspects in this
case?"

"We know Bergma's in on it," John said, and explained
his involvement in some detail, including Denise.

"Well, obviously he's your man," Victor said. "He arranged with Latour to do the job; he's the one who can exchange
the pictures at the museum in Amsterdam. Rashid couldn't do
that. Besides, he has an alibi. It has nothing to do with Rashid."

"Except that Rashid was in the Netherlands at the time the
deal was arranged, and he's here now," John reminded him.

"Buying an office tower," Victor pointed out.

"You didn't see the look the sheikh gave Bergma when he
first saw him," I said. "And the way Bergma turned to stone.
There was definitely something in the air between them."

"The sheikh only looks as if he's glaring," Victor said.
"It's those dark eyes, a little hooded, you know what I mean?
The man's shy. Some surprising people are. Prince Charles is
shy, shyer than Di. A glare, is that all you have against him?"

"That and the coincidence of place," John said. "And the
fact that someone with Rashid's kind of money is obviously
the buyer. Oh, and the Persian dagger that was used."

"He'd hardly leave behind such an obvious clue."

"We figure the guy had to leave in a hurry. Maybe someone
was coming."

"He took time to get the pictures though, and the slides and
so on," I reminded John. "Or maybe Bergma took the slides."

"He'd do that first. That's why he was there," Gino suggested. "He got the goods from Latour; then iced him."

Victor shook his head, unconvinced. "The sheikh's kind of
money doesn't have to nickel and dime it."

Gino listened, and added, "Ayesha's beginning to look like a good suspect to me."

Again Victor talked it down. "She has a hand into one of the biggest bank accounts in the world. The sheikh would give her a couple of million if that's all she wants."

"He never gives her cash, just things. She wants to leave him," I announced. "But if you've decided to consider a woman, how about Denise Painchaud?"

"I think she was just a fling, for Latour and Bergma," John said. "They wouldn't trust an airhead in a deal of this size. If she suspected anything, she only knew the deal from this end. There's still a third man, the potential buyer. I don't want to let him get away. It's got to be somebody with a fat bank account. That lets Ayesha out. Rashid's only hold on her is money. He wouldn't give her cash and let her get away."

Victor tossed up his hands in despair. "It doesn't make any sense. The thing can't be done without Bergma, yet the pictures were stolen from him. He's lying. He's got them."

"Who would he be telling they were gone, except the buyer?" John countered. "And why would he tell the buyer a lie? If he doesn't sell the paintings, he doesn't make his money. I don't see him lying about that, not to the buyer."

"Why would the buyer steal them?" Victor asked. "He can't do the exchange at the museum. He needs Bergma."

"That's exactly my point," John said. "There's an extra person floating around. Who is he, and what's his game?"

"I need a drink," Gino said, and lifted his glass to catch the waiter's eye.

We all puzzled silently over it for a minute. "What makes sense," I suggested, "is that a third party, Ms. Painchaud, found out somehow and tried to cut herself in midway through the deal. She might have seen the pictures at Latour's studio. She wouldn't have to be a genius to recognize a Van Gogh and suspect something when she saw *ten* of them. She killed Latour, stole the pictures, and now she'll sell them to Bergma. He'll have to get the money from the third party, who probably *is* the sheikh, even if he is rich enough to buy originals. When Bergma warned the sheikh not to be in touch with him, he— Bergma I mean—kept in contact via letters or messengers or something. And this afternoon the sheikh had Ayesha smuggle a note to Bergma at the museum.''

"But why would he use Denise as a go-between?" John asked.

"Maybe she overheard the call and intercepted the message when Ayesha arrived. Told Ayesha she was to take the note, something like that."

There was some deep frowning. Victor was the first to speak. "By George, she's got it."

I glowed all over. "John, what do you think?"

"Denise has an alibi for Latour's death. And she was with me when Bergma got that call from the third party."

"But it was the sheikh that Bergma was talking to," I pointed out. "He told him the paintings were gone because they *were* gone. About her alibi, she obviously has a helper. She's through with Latour and Bergma. She has a new boyfriend."

"If she has, she isn't seeing much of him," Gino announced. "She's been followed too."

"Her phone isn't bugged though," John mentioned. "It's possible that Denise and a sharp boyfriend are behind it, but it's complicated. I like simple solutions."

I sighed wearily. "Sorry we can't oblige you."

"Admit it, Weiss. She's right," Gino said. "What none of you seems to be worrying about except me is what was in that letter Denise intercepted. Maybe Rashid set a time to make the exchange—cash for the paintings. Only who'll show up is Hot Buns, not Bergma."

John said, "If you're right, we should be hearing soon." He calmly took a bite of his roast beef. "The sheikh is being followed. If Denise meets him, we'll know. It just doesn't feel right to me. Denise isn't a bright girl. I doubt if she'd be smart enough to pull this off, a deal this size."

"All she'd have to do is air her suspicions to some sharp boyfriend. Maybe an art student, since she mixes with that crowd," Gino suggested.

"But murder?" John tugged at his mustache. "She went to a convent. She has a crucifix in her apartment."

"With all those boyfriends, she can't be too religious," I said.

"The woman's a tart," Gino announced.

"All the fashionable French women look that way to WASPs," Victor said.

"I'm not a WASP. The name's Parelli. I'm a Wop, same as you, Mazzini, and I say she looks like a tart."

"When can I meet her?" Victor asked, and laughed. "I have a sweet tooth, you know."

"What did you think of the sheikh's woman?" Gino asked.

"Beautiful, elegant, and cold as the north wind. Did somebody say she made blue movies?"

"I managed to get hold of one," Gino said, with a lascivious grin. "*Lotus Flower*." I remembered Ayesha's stunned look when the actor at the cocktail party had used that phrase. "I haven't been able to see it yet. I'm visiting Ma for Christmas. I'll give you a buzz when we get back to Toronto."

Victor, the hypocrite, said, "You shouldn't take a thing like that into your mother's house, Gino. Bring it along to the hotel. I'll guard it for you."

"I checked it at the desk," Gino grinned.

Shining Italian eyes exchanged a smile. You never saw two grown men gobble down the rest of a superb meal so swiftly. They soon darted off to get him the film.

"The rooms don't have VCRs," I smiled, after they left.

"The concierge will get them one," John said. "I really should go with them. There might be a clue in the movie."

I pinned him with a sapient eye. "Like a message tattooed on her naked body, perhaps? There won't be anything useful there. She did those movies before she met up with Rashid."

"I mean names—a producer—or maybe a face I'd recognize. Some kind of connection."

I took a long sip of coffee to give myself time to dream up a deterrent. Dare I mention giving a friend a call to pass the rest of the evening? He'd know I didn't mean female friend. No, I wouldn't resort to blackmail.

"I'll just go on up to bed then. I am pretty tired. I thought we might have an hour or so alone together, since we have to keep that adjoining door locked while Victor's here. But I don't want to be in the way of your work. You go ahead."

John sat, worrying his lip. "I guess Gino'd recognize any interesting names or faces as well as I would. Probably better."

"Are you sure? I really don't mind," I said, with such convincing sincerity I even surprised myself.

John finished his coffee. His eyes were turning liquid with desire. "That's all right. As you said, we have to be on our best behavior when your uncle's around. And I can always have a look at the movie tomorrow morning."

My patience broke. "You pervert! You damned lecher! All you want is to look at those pictures of Ayesha cavorting around naked. Don't try to con me it has anything to do with the case!"

His lips stretched in a grin. "Gotcha! Don't you try to con *me* you don't give a damn. Come on upstairs. We're wasting valuable time."

CHAPTER 15

The next morning, affairs at the hotel had resumed their normal course. While Victor had breakfast, John and I read newspapers in the lobby. Then we reversed watching posts. The sheikh darted out of the hotel, briefcase in hand, at nine o'clock, into his waiting limo. At ten, Madame Feydeau arrived for Ayesha's daily session with the tarot cards. No one had to follow Ayesha that morning. She spent the next two hours in the beauty shop, getting her hair and nails done.

By noon, we were all impatient with waiting and were becoming edgy. It was a very unsatisfying way to spend the day before Christmas. I wanted to hop in that luxurious big Caddie and drive home to Maine with John. Outside, a few languorous snowflakes fell hesitantly to the ground. Just enough to give the Christmas look. Busy shoppers jostled along, encumbered with bags and boxes. The keepers of the red kettles rang their bells, and from shop doorways the nostalgic sound of carols sung by choirs wafted on the air.

No one was a bit hungry by lunchtime, but we went to the dining room anyway, to give ourselves an excuse to stay downstairs.

"Dammit, they've got to make their move soon. They're supposed to be spending Christmas with the Staynors in the Laurentians," John worried.

"We'll just have to follow them up there," I said.

Victor wasn't much good at biding his time. When he had

finished lunch, he said, "If you don't need me, John, I believe I'll just step out and do my Christmas shopping."

John didn't try to detain him. We ordered yet another cup of coffee. "It's nice to see Victor again," John said. "He's helped a bit too."

"He found out where the sheikh is going for his ski trip."

John pulled back his shirt cuff and looked at his watch. "One-thirty. How come Ayesha hasn't hit the streets for more shopping?"

"Maybe she's wrapping Christmas presents or packing." I found myself wondering what she would give Rashid for Christmas. What did you give a man who gave you a Rolls-Royce? And what would John give me? Whatever it was, I knew that darned Van Gogh book under my sofa would be inadequate. Victor had already given me my present, an envelope, containing a hundred of the most welcome dollars I'd ever seen. I wanted to get something more meaningful for John with part of it, say half. "Or maybe the Rolls is being delivered this afternoon. She wouldn't want to be away when it came. I wonder if they'll drive it to the Staynors."

"It looks like we're going to be stuck here for Christmas eve," he said. "They may not be leaving till tomorrow. Rashid just said they're spending a Christmas holiday with the Staynors. Christmas is a Christian feast. It probably doesn't mean much to Rashid and Ayesha."

"Just another excuse for a present for her," I nodded.

John set down his coffee cup in a way that suggested his patience had broken. "I'm going to call Gino," he said.

"To get a location on Staynor's chalet?"

"Why the hell should we spend Christmas at some ski lodge? I thought we'd have all this wrapped up long ago. I'm going to call Bergma and try to get things moving, but first I should let Gino know. He said he was having lunch with his mother. I'll try him there."

He placed the call, then said to me, "Gino's coming over to discuss it."

"What will you say to Bergma?" I asked.

"That's what I have to talk to Gino about. I'd like to put it to him, point-blank. We know exactly what he's up to, and have enough evidence to get him barred from ever holding a museum post again, if not to put him behind bars. He might be willing to cut a deal, give us the paintings and the name of the buyer for immunity. I figure Gino'd go for that—providing Bergma isn't the one who arranged to have Latour iced. If he'll give evidence against Rashid, we can be out of here in a matter of hours."

"We could go home tonight! To my home, I mean. Oh do it, John. This is a lousy way to spend Christmas, with no tree or anything."

I never thought I'd hear myself describe a life of luxury at the Ritz as miserable, but that's the way I felt. Some things do take precedence over mere luxury. Christmas was definitely one of them.

He gave an understanding smile and squeezed my fingers. "I'll jawbone Gino into it; don't worry. Since your uncle's out, shall we sneak upstairs and enjoy his absence?"

We enjoyed a few minutes' togetherness, which was soon interrupted by Gino's arrival. He had reverted from last night's relative elegance back to his Eskimo parka.

"Boy, did you miss a doozer last night, Weiss!" he exclaimed. "That Ayesha, she's got a pair of—"

"Would you like a drink, Gino?" John asked hastily. He knew the magic words to shut him up.

"My veins could do with some alcohol. It might get the blood flowing again. Oh, by the way, I got a fix on the Staynors' place. It's miles from the Searles', where Bergma's going. You practically can't get there from here. There's nothing commercial for miles. It's tucked into the mountains. I don't know how they ever got the place built."

"There must be a road, or how do the Staynors get there?" I asked.

"There's a private road, but what excuse can we come up with for being on it?" Gino asked. "It's got 'No Trespassing' signs posted all over."

Cross-country skiing came to mind, only to be suppressed. Our aim was to convince Gino to finish the case today. John and I exchanged a secret smile behind his back.

John said, "Then we better take care of it before the sheikh leaves."

Gino nodded. "That might be best. I knew a free trip to a

ski lodge was too good to be true. He could toot out of there in a chopper, hop on his private jet, and be gone before we ever found out what happened. So you'll call Bergma and put a firecracker under his butt?''

''I was thinking of a bomb,'' John grinned, and reached for the phone.

John has an excellent memory. He had memorized the unlisted number. The phone rang, and rang, and rang again—eight times in all. ''He's not home,'' John said in disgust, and hung up. He tried the museum. He wasn't there either.

''If he was doing anything he shouldn't, I'd have heard from my man,'' Gino said. ''Patience, Weiss.'' He eyed the Johnnie Walker, but apparently thought he'd need his wits about him and didn't touch it.

John repeated the call at ten-minute intervals for a while. At two-thirty, he finally got an answer. I was bursting with curiosity to hear how he'd handle the call. It was kind of an anticlimax.

''You don't know me, but my name's Weiss, John Weiss,'' John said. The charade was over then. He was no longer Sean Bradley, oil tycoon. ''I'm calling about a set of slides and some notes that have come my way. Does the name Vincent mean anything to you?''

There was a splutter from the other end of the line. ''Forget it, Bergma, you're in it up to your eyeballs, and if you want to get out with your skin in one piece, you better listen to me. We'll meet at the bar of the Ritz in twenty minutes.'' Another splutter, more subdued this time. ''So take a cab,'' John said, and hung up.

He turned to us. ''His battery's shot. Left the lights on last night.''

''No, he didn't. It's an excuse,'' Gino said.

''Probably. He didn't sound real happy to hear from me. Or with the watering hole I chose for the meeting. I wonder why he's afraid to let Rashid see him.''

''That is funny,'' I said. ''He's the one who told Rashid not to get in touch with him. Maybe he's afraid the sheikh will say something . . .''

''He knows we know about the forgery now,'' John mused. ''The only thing he can be trying to hide is how Latour died.

Murder is more serious than art fraud. That's what he's jumpy about. Rashid must know, and it must involve Bergma. Let's speak to Export A and have him notify us if the sheikh gets any calls. This might be enough to rattle Bergma into indiscretion.''

I asked Export A to come up, and before long, he was at the door. "Merry Christmas, folks," he beamed. "What can I do you for?"

"Fifty bucks, if you bring us good news," John said, and pulled a couple of bills from his wallet.

"For that kind of bread, I'll make up news." John outlined the situation. Export pocketed the money and left.

It wasn't five minutes before he was back. "You must be a mind reader, man," he said, shaking his head. "A dude called Bergma called the sheikh's room. Ayesha told him the man was out. Expected back in an hour. She'd have him call."

"Bergma won't be at home in an hour. He'll be here!" I exclaimed. "He's up to something, John."

He smiled benignly. "That was the general idea."

"It's nearly twenty minutes. You'd better go down to the bar to meet him. Is Gino going?"

The men exchanged a look. "Do we really want this to be official?" John mused. "He doesn't know the cops know. I should do some fishing first. If he believes I'm working alone, he'd be more talkative."

"As an insurance investigator?" Gino asked.

"Sure, why not? I gave him my real name. I have to have some reason for knowing and for being involved. I'll hint I might keep quiet if he gives me the forgeries and drops the deal. And of course tells me who the buyer is. It's worth a shot."

"Then how are we going to get any evidence against him?" Gino demanded.

"If he has those forgeries, that ties him to Latour's murder," John said.

"He better have, because the slides and box and notes were clean, except for your prints."

"He'll holler if he thinks he can save his own skin," John said.

"It's known as honor among thieves," I added. "But what

if he doesn't have them? I still favor Hot Buns. She—''

"If he doesn't have them, he has a damned sight better idea who does have them than we have," John said. "He's the key. Nobody can substitute the forgeries for the originals but Bergma. We'll follow him and see what he does, and who he does it with."

John straightened his tie and said, "Wish me luck."

I suddenly felt as if the bottom had fallen out of my stomach. "What if he has a gun?" I asked.

"Murder isn't allowed at the Ritz," Gino said.

John laughed and lunged out of the door. "Gino, follow him," I said. A hysterical lady had suddenly invaded my body. "Bergma might pull a gun on him and force him into a car or something. We can't let him go alone."

"Don't worry. Weiss can handle himself."

"If you're not going, I am," I said. I snatched up my purse and ran wildly toward the door.

Gino grabbed my arm. "Do you want to screw up the whole deal?"

"Yes!"

I was in the hall, with Gino running after me. My legs were longer. I reached the elevator first. He followed me in, still dissuading.

"We'll just sit at a table near them and watch," I said.

"Bergma'll recognize you."

"I'll wear dark glasses." I fumbled in my purse and put them on.

"Oh jeez, that'll just call attention to you. You can't wear dark glasses in a bar. It's as dark as night in those places."

"Then he won't be able to recognize me."

"Christ, I thought John said you were bright."

Bergma hadn't arrived yet when we entered the bar. John was there, waiting for a waiter, or his order. There were quite a few people already enjoying the happy hour. John didn't speak, but he spotted us and gave a chilling stare. Gino tossed his shoulders in apology and headed for a far corner. I let him go ahead, but I sat at the table closest to John's, with my back to him. Gino eventually came back and sat with me.

"Are you nuts? This is too close, Newman."

"All he'll see is my hair. I want to be close in case you have to shoot Bergma."

The waiter came. "Two Perriers," Gino said.

"I believe I'll have a—a daiquiri instead." I needed some false courage, and wanted it in a small glass, to make rapid consumption easier.

The waiter nodded and left. "I thought we all agreed on soda water," Gino grouched.

But now that Gino was here, I thought he was glad. He watched the door like a hawk. Bergma arrived about five minutes after the daiquiri, which was now no more than a memory and a burning sensation in my throat. I heard John's chair scrape as he got up to signal him to the table.

"Mr. Weiss?" Bergma asked. I couldn't see him, of course, but I recognized the lightly accented, polite voice.

"That's right. Have a seat. You and I are going to have a little talk." John's voice sounded friendly enough, but there was a steely edge to it that meant business.

Gino grinned at me. "Bergma's seen the light. Now he's going to feel the heat. I wouldn't want to be in his shoes."

"Are you a cop?" Bergma demanded.

"No."

I assumed John had flashed his insurance I.D. Bergma said, "Oh, I see." There was a noticeable sound of relief in his voice. "What's on your mind, Mr. Weiss?"

"Saving my company money, any way I can."

"But there's no insurance fraud in—involved."

"We can speak quite frankly, Mr. Bergma," John said. "I know the deal." He outlined it succinctly, omitting any mention of Denise. Bergma didn't confirm it, but he didn't bother denying it either. "You might get clean away with it. On the other hand, it'll probably come to light sooner or later that the museum sold forgeries. That's when my company takes a scalding. And that's why I want you to hand Latour's forgeries over to me. Now you wouldn't want me to give you to the cops instead, would you?"

Bergma's reply sounded strangled and very sincere. "I don't have them!" he croaked. "They were stolen from Latour's apartment the very day I was supposed to pick them up."

"And deliver them to . . . ?"

"That's irrelevant," Bergma said, voice firming again.

"The hell it is. I want a name, Bergma, or I hand you over, *now*. Who was the buyer?"

Bergma's reply was too low to hear. "That's what I figured," John said. "A suspicious coincidence, Rashid being in Amsterdam at the right moment, and now showing up here."

"But he wasn't supposed to come here! He was supposed to meet me in Amsterdam in January. I'm beginning to think he killed Latour and stole the paintings himself. The brass knife, that seems his style. I read about it in the papers. Poor Yves. He was a gentle man, a good man. He wouldn't harm a fly. Killing him wasn't necessary. And who's next? Me? It must have been Rashid—except that he can't finalize the deal without me. And he certainly isn't interested in keeping the copies."

"What did he say when you told him?" John asked.

"We haven't discussed it." I thought John would mention the note Ayesha took to the museum, but perhaps he wanted to keep that from Bergma. "He read of Latour's murder in the papers, of course," Bergma continued. "There was no mention of the paintings. We met at the Art Nouveau Show, but you know that. You were there, with a young lady. I wanted time to think, to try to recover the paintings before meeting with Rashid. After I thought about it for a while, I realized there couldn't be anyone else who could have done it. He was the only one who knew that Latour was doing the forgeries."

"What about Ms. Painchaud? I understand she used to see Latour."

"That little fool? She wouldn't recognize a Van Gogh if she saw an original." When he continued speaking, he had begun to change his mind about Hot Buns. "Unless Latour told her— I doubt if she could have done it alone. Maybe she's got a new boyfriend."

"Nobody's been in touch with you, trying to sell the forgeries back?"

"Not a word. I've been on thorns, expecting a call. It was almost a relief when you phoned. You've got to help me, Mr. Weiss. I'll do anything. Anything you say. If the museum ever found out, I'd be ruined. Art is my life. I don't know why I ever let myself be talked into this. My life has been hell. Latour kept raising the price for his part in it—he was furious when

Denis stopped seeing him, of course. It must be Denise—Denise or the sheikh."

Even without looking, I knew Bergma was ringing his white hands. His sensitive face would be haggard. I wanted to look, but restrained myself.

"How much was he giving you?" John asked.

"Ten million."

"That much!"

"The originals are worth twenty times that! It's a gift."

"You mean a steal, don't you?"

"Very funny!"

"I wonder why neither of us is laughing," John said ironically.

"Well, what should I do? Are you going to tell the police?"

"Not yet. But I suggest you cancel that ski trip you mentioned."

"Ms. Newman—she's a friend of yours?"

"I know her slightly. I'm afraid I picked the poor girl's brains to learn what you'd told her. She's not involved. Where was it you planned to stay in the Laurentians?"

"With the Searles."

"I see. Do you happen to know the Staynors?"

"Slightly. They have some inaccessible lodge. They're not sociable at all, but they donated some old Wedgwood to the museum. You're not suggesting they—"

"I'm not suggesting anything—except that you cancel your ski trip. And call me if anyone else gets in touch with you, or if you think of anything that might help."

"It's all so bloody senseless!" Bergma exclaimed, in deep anguish. "Those paintings are no earthly good to anyone but me. I begin to think Latour was killed by an ordinary burglar."

"The burglar didn't take anything but the forgeries."

"Yes, that's the whole problem."

"How did you know they were gone, since it wasn't in the papers?"

Bergma answered in a weak, confused voice. "Latour called me the afternoon that the paintings were ready. I was to pick them up that evening. I went as soon as I left work at six-thirty. When I got there, the door was open and Latour was dead. I went in to grab the paintings. He kept them under his bed. They were gone. I got my slides and notes. Nothing else had been disturbed. After I thought about it, I began to realize it must have been Rashid.''

So Bergma had got there before us, unnoticed by Menard. "That's all for the moment," John said. "You'll be hearing from me. Oh, and thanks for the drink. You won't forget the bill?" I heard Bergma's chair scrape. "Merry Christmas," John called.

Bergma lacked either the heart or the courage to tell him to go to hell. I thought we might join John, but he got up and walked out without acknowledging our presence, and we followed him up to our room a moment later.

John exploded when he saw us. His wrath was directed mostly at Gino. "Why the hell did you bring Cassie down there?"

"Bring her? Wild horses couldn't hold her back! I followed to try to keep her from wrecking the whole show."

"It's my fault," I confessed.

Now it was my turn. "You could have queered the deal," John said, trying to glower, but his heart wasn't in it. I clung to his hands and batted my eyelashes shamelessly. "I can't have you pitching yourself into my business like this, Cassie. It could have been dangerous."

"I know. That's why I had to go. I thought he might have a gun. And we didn't know then that Bergma's such a wimp."

The argument fell to the ground. "You said it," Gino sighed. "I was afraid he was going to start blubbering. We can strike him off our list of murder suspects. He wouldn't have the guts to kill a marshmallow."

John's eyes narrowed. "He had the wits to engineer this deal."

"Did you get the impression he was playacting?" I demanded. "We couldn't actually see him. He sounded sincere."

"He sounded scared shitless," Gino modified, in his own inimitable way.

"That's exactly the way he looked," John said. "I don't think he's a violent man. I don't think he even condones violence. He was appalled at Latour's murder."

"We're no further ahead than when we started," Gino said wearily.

John considered it a moment. "We're pretty sure Bergma hasn't got the forgeries. We have our corroboration that Rashid was the third party. Ten million—maybe even the sheikh would kill for that much money. I figured two, three tops. What we haven't got is the paintings. Rashid must have them, but sooner or later he has to contact Bergma to make the switch. He can't handle that alone. We just have to be patient."

"You'll have to be patient without me," Gino said, picking up his hooded jacket. "I promised Ma I'd help make the stuffing for the turkey. I'm supposed to be taking home three loaves of stale bread. You can reach me there if you need me, John. And if I don't see you guys tomorrow, Merry Christmas, eh?"

"Oh, I have a feeling we'll be seeing you before then," John said.

CHAPTER 16

Export A was on the qui vive belowstairs. He phoned up around four-thirty and said, "She just arrived—in a brand-new Rolls-Royce Corniche. She drove it herself and had it parked in the hotel parking garage. That means the parking valet has the keys. Want I should frisk the wheels?"

"Yes, please. Especially the trunk. Let us know right away." The pictures could have been put in since we had it checked.

"You got it, Mama."

I told John. "She drove it? I thought it was supposed to be delivered."

"If she'd stopped off at Bergma's place, Menard will know."

"Right. He should be phoning any minute now."

Menard must have run to the closest phone. He called within minutes. John spoke to him, hung up, and said, "Ayesha took the new car for a little cruise around town, that's all."

"She didn't cruise toward the museum or Bergma's place?"

"No, Menard said she just drove around without stopping. She didn't go near Westmount. In fact, he thinks she was lost. He says she drove east of St. Laurent. Mean anything to you?"

"The French district. Really French, I mean. It's a joke that the Anglos who were born in the city have never been east of St. Laurent."

John shrugged his shoulder. "It's easy to lose your bearings

153

in a strange city. Rashid should be returning soon. He can't
be doing anything interesting or we'd have heard."

Export A would let us know when Rashid returned. Gino
had spoken to the switchboard operator and arranged to have
any calls to the sheikh's rooms recorded as well. It was Export
A, however, who phoned us about fifteen minutes later.

"A call just came in for the sheikh," he said in an excited
voice. "Ayesha took the message. Said he'd be back at five.
The guy asked him to call 487–8321."

When I told John, his face glowed like a tropical sunrise.
"That's Bergma's unlisted number," he said softly. "It's starting to break. I'd better give Gino a buzz and get him over here.
We don't want him stuffing a turkey when the shooting be-
gins."

He made the call, trying to sound cool, but anyone who
knows him well could hear the suppressed excitement.

When Sheikh Rashid entered the hotel about half an hour
later, Export A called to tell us. John came to rigid attention.
"This could be it. If Bergma was telling the truth, Rashid
should call him as soon as Ayesha gives him the message."

"Export A will tell us if he returns Bergma's call."

We sat, watching the minutes tick away on our watches. "It
shouldn't have taken him this long," John worried.

"Rashid will want time to think, make plans. He may not
even phone from here."

In nine and a half minutes, there was a tap at the door,
sending us both up from our chairs as if a high-powered charge
of electricity had gone through them. It was only Gino.

"This better be important," he scowled. "If I don't get that
stuffing made, we'll be eating a dry bird tomorrow."

"It's important," John assured him, and filled him in. "It's
a good thing we kept you out of it, Gino. Bergma would have
suspected the phone was bugged if he'd known the cops were
involved."

The phone rang again. This time three of us were lifted from
our seats. I answered. "Hello."

"Cass, Victor here. You'll never guess who I ran into in
Ogilvy's. Charlie Hunter, out doing his last-minute shopping."

"Who's Charlie Hunter?"

"The A and R man for Cosmos records. He wants to discuss

a deal with me. He suggested we do dinner tonight. You and John can get along without me?''

Getting along without him seemed a superb idea. ''Of course. You just enjoy yourself.''

I hung up as soon as decently possible. We didn't want the line tied up. ''Just Victor,'' I explained.

We waited some more, as the last rays of afternoon faded and night set in, early at the end of December. By five o'clock, it was completely dark outside, except for the reflection of street lights. It was a strange way to spend Christmas Eve. If we left right now, we'd be home by midnight, but it was becoming increasingly clear we wouldn't be leaving at all soon. I hadn't got John's new present or even picked up the old one in my apartment. Of course he'd understand.

At five-fifteen the phone rang again, shattering the uneasy tedium of our vigil. John took it this time. It was Export A. He listened and said, ''Good work. Keep it up.''

As he set down the receiver, his eyes lifted. They were radiant. ''Twelve midnight, on top of the mountain,'' he said. ''I hope one of you knows where that is.''

''Whereabouts on top of the mountain?'' Gino demanded.

''He means the hill in Mount Royal, where kids ski and sled,'' I interpreted. ''It should be thoroughly deserted at midnight on Christmas eve.''

''So, what's going down?'' Gino demanded.

''The sheikh and Bergma are meeting. Export A says Ayesha gave the message. The sheikh was taking a shower.''

''Cool bastard,'' Gino grumbled. ''Did she mention the pictures?''

''She said, and I quote, 'Rashid wants you to bring the items. He'll want to see them.' Bergma got all flustered, but they must know he has them. 'Bring them,' she said, and hung up.''

''He certainly conned us!'' I exclaimed.

''It isn't the first time,'' Gino admitted. ''I once let a dame convince me she was rushing a sick kid to a hospital. What she was doing was hustling a load of contraband cigarettes over the border—in a school van yet, half full of kids on a field trip. Cigs are about half price in the States. Taxes. A good thing I gave her a siren escort, or she'd have got away. A big, busty blonde, she was. Well, midnight. That gives me time to go home and finish my stuffing. I'll be back here at eleven. Which means I'll have to miss midnight mass. Jeez, I love midnight mass. But I'll be here. Eleven suit you, Weiss?''

"That suits me just fine, Gino. If there's any change of plans, you'll hear.''

"Don't stuff the bird till tomorrow,'' I added. "The stuffing can get tainted if you put it in the day before.''

He looked deeply wounded. "I know that! I always stuff the bird. No oysters though. Shellfish make Ma sick. I use apples and celery and onions, along with the breadcrumbs and stuff. Oh, and raisins. Very tasty, if I do say so myself.''

He left, and John and I relaxed, for about two minutes. "Victor's away for the evening,'' John said contentedly. "We've got four or five hours to ourselves. Got any ideas?''

"Shopping,'' I announced. "I haven't finished my Christmas shopping.''

He looked dumbfounded. "The stores will be closed.''

"Not if I hurry.''

I went to my room and began scrambling into my coat. John followed, grumbling. "You left it kind of late, didn't you? I've heard of last-minute shopping, but this is ridiculous.''

"I just have to get one thing.''

"Oh, you hadn't planned on Victor's being here. Well, I'll go with you.''

"No!'' I exclaimed loudly.

"Is it for me? Look, Cass, we agreed, just a token. If you haven't got around to it, it doesn't matter. Just being here with you is the best present I could have.''

"I didn't forget your present! It's at my apartment. This is something else.''

"Gino? I don't think he's planning on exchanging gifts with us. I got him a bottle of Black Label, but—''

"It's not for Gino, silly.''

"Who, then? Who else are you going to be seeing between now and Christmas?''

"Never mind.''

"I'm going with you. I don't want you out on the streets alone after dark.''

"You better stay here and mind the phone.''

"Damn, you're right. Let me call Menard. He can go with you."

"I won't go far. I'll be fine, John. Do you think I never go out alone at night when you're not here? Don't be so protective. I'll walk softly and carry a big purse." I lifted my shoulder bag to show him how big.

He pulled me into his arms. "I can't help it. If anything happened to you . . ."

I gave him a fond smile and a light smack on the mustache. "I know. You can't live without me. Except for the ninety-nine percent of the time we're on opposite sides of the ocean."

"I made a mistake, urging you to go on with your studies. No reason a lady couldn't study French at the Sorbonne . . ."

I gulped in delighted surprise. "I better go," I said, and went, mind reeling with delightful images of the only Paris I know, that seen in movies and magazines. The Eiffel Tower, l'Arc de Triomphe, Notre Dame, and last but not least, Maxim's.

In a French mood, I bought John a bottle of Yves Saint Laurent eau de toilette for men. The drugstore was closing when I went in, and they didn't have a wrapping service, so I had to get paper and ribbon too. Then, with the clerk jiggling impatiently, I remembered Victor. He hadn't mentioned receiving my present. I'd sent him a rather nifty pen and pencil set. The clerk outstared me, and I decided one present for my uncle was enough.

John was pacing the floor like an expectant father when I returned. His worried frown faded into a smile of welcome. "What do you say we order dinner in?" he asked.

"What do you mean, pizza?"

"On Christmas Eve? I meant room service. Wine, turkey, the works."

"You can't have turkey on Christmas Eve, John. You have that for Christmas dinner."

"Is it a law? I'd like turkey."

"Yes, it's a law. The anti–Christmas Eve turkey law. I'll have a pepper steak. You can pick the wine. Oh, and something from the French pastry tray. You choose. I have to wrap my present."

That took about five minutes, three of which were used to

cut a huge sheet of wrapping paper to size with my manicure scissors. The edge looked as though a mouse had gnawed through it, but I folded it under. The bow was bigger than the box. I turned on the TV while I worked, and listened to some boys' choir sing Christmas hymns. The Christmas feeling was there, just on the edge of my grasp, but not quite getting through to me. I wanted the Christmas feeling. When the present was wrapped, there was no tree to put it under.

I probably looked woebegone when I went back to the sitting room. "Sorry I messed up your Christmas, honey," he said. "Would you like to open your present now? It might put you in the mood."

I was tempted, but the strong arm of tradition held me in its grasp. "Not till tomorrow morning. Let's just sit here and listen to the Christmas carols and imagine there's a tree in the corner. I guess we could probably allow ourselves one drink, since zero hour isn't till midnight."

"I ordered wine with dinner. Let's wait. I'll tell you what, why don't you go and take a shower and put on one of those fancy dresses? Maybe that'll put you in a party mood."

I didn't want a party mood; I wanted a—*the* Christmas mood. I felt an atavistic longing for the trembling excitement of Christmases past, believing in Santa Claus, aching with impatience for him to come. It hadn't been like that for years, but the memory returned every December.

"Dinner isn't coming till seven, so you can take a nice relaxing soak if you like. I think I'll do the same," John said.

The hotel supplied little samples of assorted toiletries, including a bubble bath. I decided to indulge myself. It was strange that I thought so little about the case as I lay in the warm water, with bubbles tickling my chin. That was on hold till midnight or thereabouts. For the next half hour I just let my mind roam. It often veered in the direction of John's present for me. He already had it, and it wasn't big enough to be obvious in his room. Something small, then. A ring?

That was what I wanted. I didn't care if it was a small diamond. I didn't care if it was a zircon, just as long as it was an imperishable piece of metal I could stick on my third finger, left hand, as a symbol of our love. Or a token, if you will.

Since the white gown had had one outing, I wore the gold

one. I shimmered like sunshine on water when I stood at the mirror. Even the punishing fluorescent light over the sink couldn't completely mar the effect. It was my hair that did that, so I twisted it up behind in a swirl and used a lavish hand with the eye makeup. I wore Sherry's present again on my ears. I really loved those heavy, uncomfortable earrings. They tinkled like tiny wind chimes at my ears and looked festive.

When I was all set for my grand entrance, I opened the door and went into the sitting room. I blinked, and stared, unable to believe my eyes. It had been transformed into a perfect model of Christmas Eve. A tree, fully decorated, had grown in the corner. Beneath it lay an embarrassment of beautifully wrapped presents. Poinsettias were everywhere. Tinsel bedizened the doorway. Tears dimmed my eyes, and a mute surge of emotion swelled inside me. The boys' choir on TV was singing "Silent Night."

Through the midst of tears, I saw John, looking haggard and sweaty from his task. He hadn't taken his long soak or even changed. He had been scurrying around like a squirrel to create this miracle. I ran into his arms, blubbering like a baby. "John, how did you—where did all this come from? Oh, I feel so—"

He crushed me in his arms and kissed me into silence. What made me think I needed a ring? I had something better than cold metal. I had a sweet, caring man, one in a zillion, and an unforgettable moment I'd relive a thousand times. I dabbed at my melting mascara and just looked at him.

"You!" What could I say? "Oh John, this is too much. I feel—and I only got you a stupid book."

"Sweetheart, I don't need any present but the look on your face."

He meant it too. I didn't really need any present but the look on *his* face and the love gleam in his eyes. "I hope these aren't all for me!"

"Not all. There's something there for Victor and Export A."

"How did you *do* all this? I was only gone half an hour."

"Forty minutes. Export A and the staff did most of it. I ordered the tree and trim yesterday, and the stores wrapped the presents for me."

"But when did you buy them?"

"I picked out most of them when we went shopping for your working clothes and had Export A keep them downstairs. I noticed the things you liked but didn't buy."

"Oh lord, I feel like such a piker."

He lifted my chin and smiled into my eyes. "Hey, it's a fiancé's prerogative to load his beloved down with a bunch of foolish stuff she'll never use."

"Never use! That's what you think! If that white cashmere turtleneck is there, I may put it on and never take it off."

"Oh yeah, it's there. And the plaid slacks—"

"No, don't *tell* me!"

"Aren't you going to open them?"

"Of course I am, on Christmas morning. I have the Christmas feeling, John. And it isn't the presents. It isn't that at all. It's—oh, it sounds so corny. It's love."

"We like corn, out in Nebraska," he said, and took my hand to point out various details of the decor. "Since you're so traditional, I got all red poinsettias. They come in white and pink now too."

I squeezed his hand. "I like red best."

He squeezed mine back. "I thought you would."

The room started misting up again. "I just can't believe it. You did all this."

"I only have these few days to spoil you. This is to make up for all the dates we've missed. And all the phone calls I didn't make. I guess I got a little ticked off a while back when I called two or three times and you were out—on dates with other guys."

"Sherry didn't tell me!"

"That's because I'm a cunning rascal. I didn't tell her who was calling. I was working myself into a real lather."

"If it bothers you that much, I won't see other men."

He considered it a moment. "No, that's unreasonable. A coed wants to go to the college dances and things. Just remember who it is you love."

"I'm not likely to forget it."

Dinner arrived on a trolley, and we just stood gazing lovingly at each other while the waiter arranged it. He must have thought we were both zonked on something. We didn't say a word.

Before we ate, John poured the wine and proposed a toast.

"Merry Christmas, darlin'. I hope it's the first of many we share."

"I'll drink to that, John."

CHAPTER 17

"I wonder if Ayesha will go to Mount Royal with the sheikh," I mentioned, over coffee. John wanted to keep his head clear for business, but I was sipping a liqueur.

"He won't take a lady along. We don't really know how deeply she's in all this. She's probably just an innocent messenger."

We exchanged a certain look, a kind of contest of wills. He had refused to let me go with him; a decision not yet accepted by me. After our splendid evening, I wasn't in a mood to fight about it, but subtler persuasions might be brought to bear.

"You've got a job to do here," he pointed out. "I'll leave you the number of the car phone. You're going to phone us and let us know when the sheikh leaves the hotel. We want to be there early."

"You know perfectly well that the Mountie Gino has downstairs is going to do that. Don't patronize me, John."

"No, the Mountie's going to follow the sheikh and just make sure he goes where he said he was going. Christmas Eve, we didn't want to call in any more men than necessary. You have that phone number I gave you?" I nodded sulkily.

It was ten-thirty. John was leaving at eleven. "I wish Victor would get back before I have to leave," he worried. "I don't like to leave you here alone."

I was swift to point out, "I'll probably be in more danger here than if I were with you."

"That bone's already been picked clean, darlin'. You're staying here."

"Then I might as well get sloshed," I said defiantly, and poured myself another glass of Bailey's Irish Cream. John knows it's my weakness and had given me a bottle in one of those gifts under the tree. It was the only one I opened.

"Why not? It'll help you relax."

Our idyllic evening had been interrupted by calls to Gino and visits from Export A. It had been arranged that John would meet Gino a few blocks away, at the corner of Sherbrooke and Crescent.

"I'll have to stay awake long enough to phone you when Export A lets me know the sheikh has left though," I pointed out.

The quick look of surprise that flickered over his face told me the Mountie downstairs had been ordered to do that. John didn't say anything, but I ribbed him about it. "If the job's already been assigned to someone else, tell me."

"No, no! You phone," he insisted. "That way, I'll know you're safe."

It was a crumb to appease me. I looked at the tree, with presents all around the floor beside it, and relented. He was only making me stay here because he didn't want me to be in any danger. I knew that and appreciated it. I was only frustrated, not angry.

"Take care of yourself, John," I said softly. "What time do you think you'll be back?"

"Not before two. We'll have to take them down to the station. Don't wait up for me."

"As if I could sleep!"

We sat together on the sofa, looking at the tree and talking and kissing till it was time for John to go. Then I sat on alone, just thinking. It was so quiet you could hear the poinsettias breathe. I turned up the TV and poured myself the last cup of coffee to make sure I stayed awake. At eleven-thirty, Export A phoned up and said the sheikh had just left, alone. Ayesha hadn't accompanied him. I dutifully called Gino's car and relayed the information, fully aware that the Mountie had beat me to it, but John might worry if I didn't phone as arranged. Victor still hadn't returned. I wondered what Ayesha was doing. This would be her chance to break free of Rashid, when they arrested him. She could return half the stuff she'd bought at the store and live on that till she got work. I'd speak to Victor about the work.

When the phone buzzed ten minutes later, my heart jumped straight into my mouth. It was only Victor. "Are you still up?" he asked.

"Of course I am. Why don't you come down to my room and we'll see Christmas in together?"

"I've already changed. I'm in my pajamas. Why don't you and John come here and we'll have a nightcap?"

I didn't tell him about John's errand over the phone. "All right," I said, without giving it much thought. But when I got there, I began to worry about leaving my phone unattended and stayed only a minute to fill him in on the latest developments. I saw from outside his door that the elevator was still at his floor and hurried to catch it. I felt a rising anxiety that I was missing a call. As I rushed past Ayesha's room, she opened her door and peered out.

"Oh, it's you!" she exclaimed, smiling. "I heard someone rushing along and thought it was Rashid. He had a business meeting—at midnight on Christmas Eve. Can you imagine?" She laughed in disbelief. "He said he was going to try to find a church having midnight mass afterward. He wanted to see what it was like. He's probably meeting some woman. Why don't you come in and have a drink, Cassie?"

Ayesha wasn't in her white satin and marabou feathers tonight. She wore satin-striped lounging pajamas in various shades of rose and mauve, and looked rather lonesome. "Or are you and John—"

I duly noted what the sheikh had told her, but soon wondered whether she knew the real truth. Perhaps she just thought it was some legitimate business. If she were guiltily involved, wouldn't she have omitted the business meeting entirely and just said Rashid decided to attend a midnight mass? That sounded more plausible. She had asked about John very nonchalantly too. But most convincing of all was that remark about Rashid being with another woman.

No matter, I was too fidgety to get back to the phone to

oblige her. "I have to run, sorry, Ayesha. I'm expecting a phone call."

She looked a little offended.. After I was safely back in my room, staring at the silent phone, I remembered my decision to try to help her. Maybe I should begin by giving her an inkling that she'd soon be losing Rashid permanently. I paced the rooms, my mind in a turmoil and my stomach feeling as if it were being pinched by a giant nutcracker. I leapt a foot when a light tap came at the door. Export A, I thought, and made a dash for it. But when I looked through the peephole, I saw it was Ayesha.

She was alone and carrying a bottle of champagne. Her striped-satin pajamas fit like a glove. Obviously she wasn't armed. I hesitated, wondering what to do. She looked awfully sad. Alone on Christmas Eve, like me. I'd phone Victor and invite him to join us. A beautiful young woman not his niece would be a strong incentive. That would help pass the time till John returned. And when Ayesha heard the truth, she'd have us to help her. It was the decent, Christian thing to do. If you're ever going to heed your conscience, surely Christmas is the time for it.

I opened the door. "Me again," she said apologetically. "Did you get your phone call yet?"

"I—yes, I did, but I just have to make another call. Come on in."

She stepped in and looked all around. "Where's John?"

"He's having a meeting with his assistant. I'll just call my Uncle Victor. You remember him."

"Of course." She followed me into the sitting room and discovered the tree. "How lovely! I should have thought of doing this!"

"It was John's idea; so thoughtful of him."

"And look at all those presents! Why haven't you opened them?"

"I will, tomorrow. Why don't you open the wine and I'll call Victor."

I went toward the phone. I didn't hear any sound behind me. The first intimation I had that anything was wrong was the pressure at my back, as if someone was pushing a pencil against my spine.

"Put it down," Ayesha said, in her perfectly modulated, polite accents.

I replaced the receiver. No panic overcame me yet, just surprise, and curiosity. I replaced the receiver and turned. I can overpower her easily, I thought. She's small and out of shape. It was that little round black hole of the muzzle that sent the first tremor of fear through me. The gun was a very dainty little silver one with a darker bulge of metal on the end. A silencer? She must have had the gun hidden behind the champagne bottle, or perhaps tucked into her waistband, hiding the bulge with the bottle.

I tried to speak, but no sound came out. My throat was bone dry. I tried again, and my words came out in a squeak. "What are you doing?"

"Just tying up a few loose ends," she said, and tossed her head toward the door. "This way. Not a sound, or you're dead."

"So you *are* helping Rashid!"

She snorted. I edged my way toward the door, figuring how to escape. Once we were in the hallway, I'd turn suddenly and knock the gun out of her hand. She opened the door, and Jan Bergma slid in, sideways like a crab. His face was white and strained; his black eyes were glazed with fear.

"This'll have to be quick," Ayesha said, in a cold, businesslike voice. "They'll be back soon." She turned a sardonic smile on me. "From that imaginary little meeting at the top of the mountain I arranged for them."

"Why?" was all I could think of to say.

"Because they expected it. I didn't want them realizing Rashid has nothing to do with this. I needed time to think, to plan. This way is better. I convinced Rashid he wanted to see a Christian mass. I like to off one victim at a time. Less chance for accidents." She might have been playing a role, and relishing it. Victor had come up with the right name for her. Dragon Lady.

"But the phone calls! You said Rashid—"

"I had to talk fast, before Jan spilt the truth."

One victim at a time. My God, she intended to kill John too! And all I could think of was how much I loved him, and how sweet he'd been about arranging that Christmas tree for me. When he came back, she'd be waiting with that little silver gun . . . My insides were shaking, and a ball of fear was growing in my throat. Strangely, Jan Bergma looked even more frightened than I. He wasn't relishing any of this. If I could co-opt his help . . .

"You killed Latour?" I asked, in a shaky voice.

"His job was done—superbly. I didn't need him any longer. Why split the money three ways?"

"Is Rashid the buyer?" I asked.

"That's enough questions. Into the bedroom."

I didn't move. If she wanted to kill me in the bedroom, she'd have to force me physically to walk. I looked a mute appeal to Jan.

"Can't we just tie her up?" he asked. He began wringing his hands nervously.

"Don't be an ass. She knows everything. Find your slides and notes. They were in the sitting room last time I saw them."

"But Weiss knows everything too," he pointed out.

"He's next. Divided they fall," she said, and laughed a very strange laugh. She was high on something, not completely bombed, but definitely high. Oh God, there was no counting on rational behavior from a drugee. Maybe she wasn't as calm as she pretended. She needed that false courage actually to kill in cold blood.

How did they know John's name? He'd been masquerading as Sean Bradley. But he'd told Bergma his real name. "The police know too," I said, directing my words to Jan.

He looked even more frightened. "We can't kill cops!" he exclaimed.

"She's lying. There's just herself and the insurance investigators, Weiss and his fat assistant."

"His fat assistant is a Mountie," I said, sensing a reprieve.

"Bullshit! Mounties have to be at least five feet ten inches, and they don't hire illiterates. Do you think I'm an amateur?"

"He's a federal policeman," I insisted, though it did seem incredible.

"And I'm a saint. Into the bedroom." She pushed the gun into my face. I took a few steps backward. "Hurry up!"

I looked a plea at Bergma. "You'll be next," I warned him.

"She's already killed Latour. Now me and John. Do you think she'll leave you alive?"

Jan wiped his hand over his lips. "She can't finalize the deal without me." He was weak. One of those weak men who will close his eyes to any horror, so long as it doesn't touch him personally. I had to appeal to his own safety.

"So far you're only involved in art fraud," I said, pinning him with a stare. "You weren't there when she killed Latour. This is accessory to murder."

"Tie her up and let's get out of here," Bergma exclaimed. Perspiration beaded his brow.

"I want a clean getaway. She has to go, and Weiss and the fat man."

"You'll never get away with it," I heard myself say, with a sense of unreality. I too had become an actress in her melodrama.

"I'll get away with it all right. When they find one woman's body and two men's, they'll leap to all the wrong conclusions. Weiss will be holding the gun," she decided. "A love triangle that has nothing to do with me."

At that, she took me by the shoulder, turned me around, and pressed the gun against my back. I went into the bedroom. She flicked on the lights. This couldn't be happening. I couldn't become a victim of murder at the Ritz, on Christmas Eve. John . . .

"Take off your dress," she ordered calmly. "Let your hair down and get into bed." I began to pull out the hairpins, slowly, trying to think. "Did the tarot cards show this was going to be a bad day for you, Cassie? Or have you still not learned to read them? If you hadn't pushed your way into my life, I wouldn't have to kill you."

"Ayesha, you don't have to. Why kill me? You're not going to get away with this. Loads of people know. There's a whole army of cops following every move you and the sheikh make."

"Mostly Rashid, I think. If the cops ever do learn what's going on—and there's no reason they should—they'd never believe I could afford ten million dollars to buy the forgeries."

"If you have that much money, why are you . . . ?"

"I don't have it, you fool! I'm not the buyer."

"Then who . . . ?"

"A gentleman friend. You wouldn't know him. Now the dress."

I had removed the pins. My hair tumbled around my shoulders. "I had planned to help you," I said, hoping against hope to change her mind. "I was going to have Victor get you into movies."

"I've been in movies, thank you. I'm not interested in showing my body any longer. It's hard work, keeping in that kind of shape. Time to use my mind instead."

"I don't mean blue movies!"

"What did you have in mind? Gidget? I'm no longer interested in a film career. It's too much like work. Hurry with that dress."

I reached behind and fumbled with the back zipper, while I made a mental tour of the room. What could I use for a weapon? Hairbrush wasn't heavy enough. Shoes? A spiked heel across the temple . . . She'd make me take off my shoes before I got into bed. If I attacked her, she'd shoot. I'd have to throw one at her, and hope my aim was good. The silence stretched. To distract her, I asked, "Where did you hide the forged paintings?"

"I left them with a friend for safekeeping."

I doubted if she had a friend in the world. "How do you plan to escape?"

"With Rashid will be the best way. Once the lot of you are gone, there'll be nothing to tie him or me to all this. They're so casual with him at customs. I convinced him he didn't want to go skiing after all. We're going to London—via New York to give my Christmas present a trial run. If that zipper's stuck, just give the dress a yank. No matter if you rip it. You won't be wearing it again. And kick off your shoes. *Kick* them off. I wouldn't want you getting any foolish ideas."

A burning anger began to grow in me. I had pitied this bitch. I had wanted to help her. She didn't want to work. She just wanted money, and to shop her life away. My shoes were open-backed gold slippers. They were practically falling off, so I couldn't pretend they were tight. I shuffled out of them. The zipper, far from being stuck, unzipped itself and began to slide down past my knees. I'd soon be in my half-slip and bra.

Would she make me take everything off, to add an air of authenticity to the love triangle she had in mind?

Not content to filthy up her own life, she wanted to make her victims' deaths sordid as well. When people listened to the news tomorrow, they'd believe that John and Gino and I were involved in some sex scandal. I'd be damned if I'd let her get away with it.

"I'm becoming very impatient," she said. And she was. Her fingers clutched at the gun so nervously that she might fire it accidentally if I delayed much longer.

My gold lamé gown slithered to the floor. Before she could tell me to kick it aside, I reached down and picked it up. With a swift movement, I slashed it at the hand that was holding the gun. A muffled shot rang out and a bullet imbedded itself in the wall. I made a lunge for her, and simultaneously Jan Bergma appeared at the door.

"Grab her!" Ayesha yelled. My dress had wrapped itself around her face and neck. She clawed at it with her long, blood red nails. The thumbnail came loose and hung like a gigantic scarlet fish scale from her thumb.

Jan stood a moment in the doorway, undecided. I grabbed the gun while I had the chance and pulled Ayesha in front of me, wrenching one arm behind her back. I should have been triumphant, but I was still scared out of my wits. It was two against one, and one of the two was a strong man. Physically strong, I mean. Ayesha had enough determination and lack of scruples for anything. If they turned on me, I'd have to shoot. My heart was pumping like a steam engine inside me. Could I do it? To save my life, and John's and Gino's, I'd have to.

I spoke to Jan. "Into the other room," I said, in a voice of mock bravado. He went like a lamb to the slaughter, and I pushed Ayesha on in front of me. I had to tie them up—her first. She was the more treacherous. "Take off your tie," I ordered him. White and sweating, he undid it.

"Don't do it," Ayesha ordered. "She won't shoot me. She hasn't got the nerve."

Jan looked from one to the other. He stretched the tie between his two hands and pulled, while his black eyes studied me. I could almost feel that tie around my neck. If he tried it, I'd have to shoot him. And my trembling hand better aim straight.

"You'll go first, Bergma," I said, but it was against her spinal column that I pushed the gun.

The next bit would be tricky, to get him to tie her up. Between them, they might outwit me. At that awful moment, the phone rang. I wasn't about to be distracted by answering it. It rang six times, jarring my nerves. It seemed it would never stop. Surely someone would come soon. If it was Export A phoning, he'd come to investigate. If it had been John on the phone and I didn't answer, he'd send someone upstairs to check. It might be better just to hold the gun on them and wait, instead of having Jan tie her up.

It was less than sixty seconds before there was a banging at the door. "You all right, Cassie?" Export A called.

I did the crabwalk to the door, holding the gun aimed right between Ayesha's scheming eyes, to let him in.

He took one look and his eyes goggled. "Holy Christ! What's going down here?"

"Call the cops," I said.

"They're on their way. John just phoned, said you weren't answering the phone. He's coming back. The sheikh didn't show."

"Fine, then we'll just wait."

Export A came in. I was vastly relieved to have an ally. "Tie them up, will you?" I said, in a weak voice.

He used Bergma's tie to tie him up, and one of John's for Ayesha, while I stood guard with the gun. With their arms secured behind their backs, I could breathe easier.

"Where are the paintings?" I asked her.

She gave me a malignant look and said, "Up your ass."

Export A slanted a grin at me and said, "Funny you didn't notice."

I turned to Jan. "Bergma?"

"She took them for safekeeping. I don't know where she put them. I had no idea she was going to kill Latour." He was as talkative as Ayesha was sullen. "I didn't know till she told me. She told me tonight she took a cab to a spot near Latour's apartment and walked the rest of the way so she wouldn't be noticed. He'd never met her. She let on she was looking for the woman who used to live in his apartment, and when he went to find the address the woman had left behind, she knifed him and took the paintings. She *bragged* about it.''

"Shut up, you fool!" Ayesha snapped.

"Do you know who the buyer is?" I asked Jan.

"A Swiss businessman who used to be her lover. His name's Leopold Dornach. He has a whole castle full of artwork outside Zurich. Half of them are stolen.''

"Dornach will kill you," she warned.

"This is all your fault!" Bergma croaked, close to tears. "I never agreed to *murder*. You asked if I wanted to make a few easy million. No one would get hurt, you said!" Jan turned to me and continued, "Dornach heard about the sale at the museum and was planning to buy a few of the Van Goghs. It was her idea to have them forged and the forgeries sold in their place, Dornach getting the originals. He arranged with the Van Gogh Museum in Amsterdam for me to come here. He has immense influence. She asked me who could do the forgeries, and I fingered Latour—I knew him from Holland. She was going to get fifty percent. Latour and I shared the other five million. But she was too greedy. She killed him, and she'd have killed me too as soon as I made the substitutions.''

"Why did you go along with her?" I asked. He seemed too weak for such skulduggery.

He gave her a jaundiced look. "She came to Amsterdam and seduced me. She can be very persuasive.''

She spit at him. "Next time I'll hire a man.''

"There ain't going to be a next time, lady," Export A smiled.

At last the pounding of running feet was heard in the hallway, and John came storming in. Gino was a few yards behind him. John took one look at me, then at the gun in my hand, and finally over my shoulder to my captives. His eyes were staring, and his whole body trembled. He pulled me into his arms and squeezed me so hard my bones ached. "Thank God," he breathed in my ears, and finally let me go. His voice was shaking harder than his arms.

Gino came panting into the room, looked all around and smiled. "I told you she'd be all right, Weiss. Cassie's a smart lady. Let's face it, we fumbled the pigskin and she recovered it. Handcuff time, folks," he said, and merrily jingled a pair of cuffs from his pocket, but when he saw the culprits were tied up, he didn't bother to use them. Instead he went to the phone and called for his car.

When John recovered, he noticed I was undressed. "Maybe you'd better put some clothes on," he suggested.

I had forgotten I was in my half-slip and bra. He followed me into the bedroom, just to make sure nobody assaulted me on the way. "What happened?" he asked. "Rashid didn't show at the mountain. He left the hotel at eleven-thirty all right, but the guy following him said he went to mass. We made a stop at the church, and there he sat, just looking. Wasted ten minutes seeing who came to sit beside him. It was a pair of teenagers. So I decided I better call back here and see if you were all right. When you didn't answer . . ."

"Rashid doesn't know what's going on. She masterminded the whole thing. I was afraid they'd escape if I let myself be distracted, so I didn't answer the phone." I shimmied into slacks and a sweater. "Tell you all about it later. Let's join the party." I grabbed his hand and pulled him forward.

There were a few points I wanted to clear up, and I asked Bergma when Ayesha learned John was an insurance investigator, since there was no point asking her.

"She found some papers the day you read the tarot cards. I learned only this afternoon when I met Weiss in the bar. She never told me anything. We were afraid to meet." I interpreted that to mean he was afraid to meet her. He was the one who warned her off on the phone.

"How about yesterday afternoon when she went to the museum?"

"I saw her there, but we didn't speak. She gave Ms. Painchaud a note for me in the washroom, saying we had to meet. She said she was setting something up, and she'd call me, but for me not to call her in case her phone was bugged. After I met Weiss I *did* call her, but I was careful what I said. When she said the sheikh was out, I knew she was being cautious. I learned only tonight that she was trying to pin it on Rashid. Her phone calls didn't make any sense. I decided to risk coming to the hotel and slipping up the fire stairs to her room."

Ayesha gave a bored look in our general direction; then looked away. She didn't look frightened, or angry, or anything, just bored. But I imagine she must have been a cauldron of anger and regret inside. Perhaps she was a better actor than any of us had realized. Or perhaps she was incapable of registering emotion, even when she truly felt it.

"Someone should speak to the sheikh," I mentioned, feeling sorry for him.

"I'll take this pair downtown. You want to speak to the sheikh, Weiss?" Gino asked.

John nodded. Gino handcuffed the pair together and led them out the door, with Export A along to help keep an eye on them. I didn't think he'd be needed. Ayesha had shackled herself to the wrong helper for this job.

"Want me to go to Rashid's room with you?" I asked John.

"I wouldn't mind the company, if you have the stomach for it."

"I'll go. Worse things happen to me when you leave me behind," I reminded him.

He squeezed my hands till they ached; then gave me a gentle kiss on the lips. "You don't have to remind me, darlin'. I have enough nightmare material to last me a lifetime."

Rashid was nearly as impassive as Ayesha when John told him. His face didn't move; his eyes didn't blink. He looked inscrutable, like a Buddha.

"I had begun to suspect she no longer cared for me," he said. "You must not judge her too harshly. She was not like other women. There was a wild, headstrong streak in Ayesha. A part of her appeal. I hoped to bind her to me with—things." He gave a futile hunch of his massive shoulders. "She liked pretty things. Too much, perhaps. But she liked danger and excitement more."

"What is her background?" John asked.

"She comes from a good home. Her father was a diplomat." So she had told the truth about that, then. "She ran away from school when she was sixteen, when her mother divorced her father."

"The mother didn't commit suicide?" I asked.

"No. She was a flighty woman. That's where Ayesha gets it. She amused herself with drugs, guitar players, who knows what else? She still manages to find drugs wherever we go. They are so easily available nowadays to someone like her, with cosmopolitan connections. I refuse to give her cash, but

I suppose she sells things. Even *my* things, sometimes. A watch was missing recently and a little ornamental dagger I keep for sentimental reasons. She buys a great deal. I don't know. What will become of her?''

I didn't think she had left Rashid's dagger there on purpose to involve Rashid. That would bring suspicion too close to home. It was probably an oversight, but when she remembered it later, she put it to use.

"She'll spend a long time in prison. You don't walk away from murder," John said.

"I'll hire a lawyer; do what I can. I shall miss her." I saw, or imagined, a tear glazing his eye. "I daresay the police will want to speak to me before I leave."

"Mr. Parelli will be in touch with you tomorrow."

"Make it in the morning if possible. I am very anxious to get to London—business."

He had no crushing business in London. He had planned to go to the Laurentians until Ayesha talked him out of it. Whatever he felt for her, it wasn't love. But then he knew her better than any of us. He knew whether she was capable of being loved. He would continue footing the bills, and that was apparently all she had ever wanted from him. There seemed no point in telling him she had tried to blame it on him, though he might learn about the dagger eventually.

CHAPTER 18

Christmas morning away from home wasn't so bad. I had John and Victor, and such an abundance of presents that I felt a little like Ayesha. Victor was piqued at being left out of last night's excitement, but as there had been no media involvement, he was able to forgive us.

"So you tied up all the loose ends without me," he said, shaking his head.

"Not quite all," John said. "We still haven't found the forged paintings. Ayesha hasn't talked. Rashid hired her the most expensive lawyers in town, and they're not letting her say much."

"She said last night she left them with a friend," I mentioned, "but that's obviously not true. She doesn't have any friends here."

"Poor girl," Victor said. "Alone, friendless. No wonder she got into trouble. What would a woman like that do all day long?"

"Shop," John said.

"And have her fortune told," I added. "The only person she met all day was Madame Feydeau, and—John! Did you question Madame Feydeau? Ayesha was seeing her before we started watching the sheikh and her."

John blinked. "I must be going senile! I forgot all about her."

"Ayesha gave me Madame's phone number."

"We won't call. Madame might be more deeply involved than we think. I'll find out her address and take a run over."

"I'll go with you." He opened his mouth to object. "Instead of being left behind and nearly killed," I reminded him.

"I have a feeling I'm going to be hearing a lot about last night, in the future."

"Not if you learn the lesson fast. We'll be right back, Victor."

Madame was in the yellow pages. John got to drive the big Caddie limo, as he'd been dying to all along. Madame lived in the district called Saint Henri. It wore the traditional face of old, lower middle-class French Montreal. Duplexes with black iron stairs leading to the upper story are a feature. The houses are mostly brick, with trim painted in lively shades of orange, turquoise, or mustard. Large numbers of children used to be another feature. *La Revanche du Berceau*, they called it (The Revenge of the Cradle). Having lost the war to the English on the Plains of Abraham, they would win it by sheer numbers. Double-digit families were the rule until the pill generation. I didn't see many children in the streets.

The Caddie looked out of place, parked in front of Madame's little duplex. A sign in the lower-level window announced her calling. We went to the door and tapped. Madame was entertaining family or neighbors. Her little house was alive with people, a Christmas tree, and assorted holy pictures on the wall. A large crèche was on a hall table. The trappings of religion persisted, even though Madame was into the occult.

She was dressed in black, all six feet of her, enlivened by a vivid shawl. Free of its customary turban, her black hair was frizzed out in an Afro. Her cheeks were heavily rouged. "I'm not working today, sorry," she said, in accented English. She began closing the door with her gnarled, ringed fingers.

"Ayesha sent us to pick up the parcel she left with you," I said.

"She did? I wondered when she didn't come herself. I was afraid she'd run off and forgotten it. She's leaving today for the skiing, isn't she?"

"Yes," I said. "She's a bit rushed, and I said I'd get it."

"I won't be a moment."

She disappeared, and soon came back with a large, soft-sided suitcase. "She was afraid the sheikh would peek," she said, smiling conspiratorially. "His Christmas gift," she nodded. "I'm sure he'll love it. Did she tell you what it is?"

I smiled back. "No, she just said it was his present."

"A painting of herself. She had it done in Paris. I told her she should have it framed, but it's for the Paris apartment, and it would be easier to carry unframed. A lovely thought, wasn't it? She is a delightful woman. What an aura! So generous! I shall miss her."

She looked at the suitcase, much larger than a single canvas would require. "Of course she's giving him a few small gifts as well. One of those ski sweaters, and I think she mentioned a gold pen . . ."

My nerves were squealing to get away and open the case. "Thank you. Merry Christmas."

We drove a few blocks away before trying to open the case. It was locked, probably to prevent Madame Feydeau from snooping and discovering that the portrait of Ayesha had turned into ten forged Van Goghs. We took it to the hotel to open. Victor was still in John's sitting room, using his phone for a long distance call to Italy, where he frequently called to chat with the Contessa Carpani, to prolong the loan of her Stradivarius violin.

"Ah, I wish I could be there with you," he said. "Toronto is feet thick in snow. I would have asked you to join me, but your delicate constitution could never take it. It would be cruel to ask you to come. So I sit here alone, dreaming of you."

He took a quick sip of his Irish coffee and winked. "February?" he asked. "Delightful! Just let me check my agenda and see if I'm free." He rustled the phonebook. "Can you believe it! I'm booked up solid that month, in Los Angeles. A documentary the movie people are putting together on me. If only I had known you were coming to New York! Could you put it off till July? . . . No, of course, I understand. The Italian Renaissance Exhibition can't be rescheduled for my convenience. You must go, certainly. How about August?"

He talked on a moment longer, making excuses and feigning regret and lavishing compliments, while John pried the lock of the suitcase open with the corkscrew the hotel provided for each room. He opened it and took out a beautiful cerise mohair shawl. Wrapped inside it were the forged canvases. He spread them out on the sofa, one by one.

There was one of three cypress trees standing in a cornfield, under a blue night sky, which held either two moons, or the moon and the sun.

"A Saint Remy landscape," John said, gazing at it.

Victor finished his call and came to peer over his shoulder. "Is this what all the fuss is about? The guy has no sense of composition. The tree's growing right out of the top of the canvas, for crying out loud."

"He learned that from the Japanese prints," John said. "See how it forces our eye up. Cypresses are a sort of mystical symbol for Van Gogh, a link between earth and heaven."

"Looks more like a Freudian symbol to me," Victor said. "I'll bet the original Van Gogh fit the canvas better."

"This is an exact duplicate," John said. "I've seen the original. Amazing how Latour copied the brush stroke. You can almost feel the nervous tension, the hysteria, in the twist of those strokes. Van Gogh was in the asylum when he did the original of this. His colors are darkening again here, quite different from the palette he used at Arles."

"Let's see some of the brighter ones," Victor suggested.

John lifted out one of the bedroom pictures. It seemed to glow from the yellow of the bed, the sunlight at the window, and the deep golden floor. "I even see a little tribute to Vermeer in here," he said, pointing to the geometrical shapes of window, door, table, and a cluch of paintings on the bedroom wall. "All that geometry, especially the window, is reminiscent of Vermeer, don't you think?"

I agreed, but in fact had only a hazy idea what a Vermeer might look like. I determined on the spot that I'd start a crash course on art.

John gazed as though in a trance. "I remember reading in one of his letters to Theo that these bedroom scenes 'ought to rest the brain or rather the imagination.' But a good painting never does that. Quite the opposite."

"It does have a restful feel though," I countered. "A happy, restful feel."

"He didn't use his passion colors. Van Gogh used reds and greens to express what he called 'those terrible things, men's passions.' The real passion of his own life was his art. When he used the complementary colors next to each other, he'd call it 'a marriage.'

He turned to the painting of Mademoiselle Gachet. "Notice how he's speckled the green wall with red flecks. He wanted to marry her. The father, understandably, didn't approve."

Victor glanced at the painting of the woman and said, "Can't say I think much of the lady."

"Stick to the violin, Victor," John said.

"I may not know much about art, but I know what I like. And I like a painting that looks like what it's supposed to be. You've seen my Alex Colville? Now *there* is an artist."

"One of the best," John agreed. "He goes beyond realism. His women don't just look like a woman; they look like womanhood."

"And his dogs!" Victor grinned. His Colville was of a dog. "You can almost see the little rascal's rump swing."

John rolled up his eyes in disbelief, to hear such mild praise of one of his favorite artists.

"What will you do with these?" I asked, looking at the paintings.

"They'll have to be turned over for evidence. I wouldn't mind getting hold of a couple of them after the trial."

"Are you going to nab the Dornach guy, the one who was supposed to be buying the originals?" Victor asked. "I remember you were pretty eager to get the son-of-a-bitch."

"We were wrong about the son-of- part," I joked.

John said, "That'll depend on whether Ayesha has anything in writing. I doubt he'd have obliged her, but at least we're aware of what he's up to now, and we'll keep an eye on him. We'll get him sooner or later, for something."

It was only eleven o'clock. If we got moving, we could still be home in time for dinner. Victor stood up and stretched. "I hate to run off on you folks, but the manager of Thompson Hall has invited me to Christmas dinner."

"In Toronto?" I asked, surprised.

"That's where he lives. My flight leaves at one. I have to hustle. What are you two doing?"

I looked a hopeful question at John. He smiled and said,

"We're going to Bangor. If we hurry, we can just make it. Can you get yourself to the airport, Victor?"

"I've always made it so far. Thank you for the holiday, John. Great seeing you again. I'll be looking forward to an invitation to your wedding. Give my love to the family, Cass." He gave me a peck on the cheek, shook John's hand, and left.

"I'll pack while you get in touch with Gino," I said. "Maybe Export can arrange to have the rented coat returned."

It was an hour minus three minutes by the time the limo was at the door of the hotel. Export A had the coat. Gino had arrived half an hour earlier and finished what remained of the Johnnie Walker. When the hour ticked by, we were ready to take off.

Gino stood, huddled in his parka against the cold, carrying Ayesha's luggage with the forged Van Goghs. "I'll see what I can do about snagging one of the pics for you," he told John. "I'm not promising anything. You know the red tape."

"The one of Mademoiselle Gachet, if possible. Thanks for everything, Gino," John said. They shook hands.

"You won't forget to put in a word for me with the company?" Gino reminded him.

"Are you serious?"

Gino looked at the limo, and at me, who symbolized "woman," I suppose, and said, "Is this arctic wind freezing my ass off? You bet I mean it."

"Then start working up your résumé. They'll want to see it."

"I'll do that. I gotta go now, drop off these pics and get home to stuff the turkey. Christmas is great, isn't it? Ma loved the dishwasher. You should've seen her face. It was lit up brighter than the tree. If I know Ma, she'll wash the dishes before she puts them in. Well, I'll let you go now. Just one thing . . ."

I looked out the window and saw he was coming closer to me. He grabbed my chin and pulled my head out of the window, and placed a loud smack on my lips. "I've been wanting to do that for a long time. Merry Christmas, Newman."

I suppressed the urge to have my lips sterilized and managed a frosty, "Same to you, Parelli."

He was still standing on the curb, waving and grinning, with the suitcase in his hand when I looked around.

"He just blew his job with the company," John said, and laughed.

"My apartment isn't much out of the way," I explained. We were going there to pick up my presents for the family and my book on Van Gogh for John. I had already given him the cologne. The car wreaked of it. I threw the unwrapped book on top of the bag, changed out of Sherry's lovely coat and into my own less fashionable "good" camel's hair, and we left.

The snow crunched under the tires. On the streets, every breath people expired turned the air into balloons of steam. But inside the car, it was warmly luxurious. We were going home for Christmas. We still had a few days together.

"I wonder what'll happen to Ayesha and Jan," I mused.

"I can't feel too cut up about them. At least they deserve their fate. They were only thinking of themselves. I keep thinking of Vincent."

"You keep calling him Vincent, as if you were on a first-name basis."

"You kind of feel that way after you've read his diaries and letters. He's the one I feel sorry for. All he wanted was to do good, to help people, and look at his short, pitiful life. Everything turned out wrong for him. The Gauguin live-in didn't work out; he cut off his ear as a gesture of repentance. He didn't get the girl, and he didn't get a scrap of recognition when he was alive. And just when he was starting to make it, he couldn't take it any longer and killed himself. Only thirty-seven. I'm over thirty. I'm not going to make that mistake."

"I had no idea you were contemplating suicide!"

"No, just marriage." He patted his vest pocket. I noticed a suspicious bulge, about the size of a ring box.

I poked his ribs with my elbow. "You prefer a slow death."

"I'm going to grab the good times while they're going. You and me, we're going to enjoy our lives, Cass. Which reminds me, I promised you the fur coat if we cracked this case. What kind do you want?"

"No furs till we're married." I nestled into the deep luxury of the limousine and snuggled against his arm. "Let the good times roll."

"What do you say we go for a diamond instead, as in ring?"

His right hand left the wheel and he slid out the box, a little blue velvet one. While he was still driving, he pressed the lid and it popped open. I found myself blinking at a huge emerald-cut diamond. He shoved it at me. I took it, literally speechless. I heard a deep sigh of bliss hover on the air. "Well, do you like it?" he asked warily.

"Stop the car, John."

"Is that a yes or a no?"

"Stop the car."

He pulled over to the side of the road and examined me with a worried eye. My expression of undiluted bliss reassured him. "I say yes," I whispered in a trembling voice, and kissed him. "Yes, yes, yes."

"I want those McGill jocks to know you're taken."

It was quite a bit later when we turned on the radio and heard Bing Crosby moaning "White Christmas," as the miles of snow slipped by beyond the window. It was the best Christmas ever. I didn't care if we never got home. I was with John. I *was* home.